P9-CCC-649

Brinkman

Brinkman

RON GOULART

DOUBLEDAY & COMPANY, INC.
GARDEN CITY, NEW YORK
1981

All of the characters in this book are fictitious, and any resemblance to actual persons, living or dead, is purely coincidental.

Library of Congress Cataloging in Publication Data

Goulart, Ron, 1933–
Brinkman.

I. Title.
PS3557.O85B7 813'.54 AACR2

FIRST EDITION

ISBN: 0-385-13648-X
Library of Congress Catalog Card Number 78-18135

PRINTED IN THE UNITED STATES OF AMERICA

"Pray, Selim, was there any truth in that history of the princess? I thought at first that it was all invention; but when you wept—"

"That was for the sake of effect," answered the renegade: "when I get warmed with my story, I often work myself up to a degree that I almost believe it myself."

Frederick Marryat,
The Pacha of Many Tales

Brinkman

CHAPTER 1

Two events of some interest occurred on the eve of my twentieth birthday. I attended my mother's funeral, unexpectedly, and I saw my long-dead sweetheart flying about alive and affluent.

There's a possibility, the way things have been shaping up, that no one will ever read this account. In fact, there may not be anyone around to punch out a copy on his or her bookbox. More on that later.

Hell, though, I wouldn't be writing down this account of my life, or what I believed to be my life, if I really anticipated no one would ever see it. So let's be optimistic, which is what Piper is continually advising me. You don't know Piper yet, but you will.

For you possible future readers, then, I'm going to commence, as I already hinted, on the day before I turned twenty. I celebrated, though that's not quite the word, that particular birthday in January of the year 2033 and in the Connecticut Territory. Not in New Haven Citistate, which is where I'd been hoping for several years to be residing long before I grew as old as twenty, but in Nabe 13 of the Citistate fringe. My name was Justin Brinkman, or so I then supposed. More on that later.

During Shift 3 on that bitter-cold January afternoon I was flat on my back under a sparse pseudodown quilt with one leg entangled with those of somebody else's wife and the other thrust out into the chill air of her apartmentette. I'm very good at plucking up things with my toes, which I'll explain about later. While lying there drawing warmth from plump naked Heather Beasacker, age twenty-six, I was using the agile toes of my left foot to pick the pocket of her one-piece worksuit, flung on the frigid floor during an earlier moment of abandon.

To lull Heather's not overly suspicious mind I was caressing her most accessible breast. She was one of those girls who prefer nearly absolute silence during and immediately after an encounter. Fine with me in this case, since I could concentrate on getting her Grub chits out of her pocket and hidden in my boot.

Heather, not a bad-looking girl as I recall though dangerously close to having two chins, was spread out with her hands locked behind her head and her eyes staring ceilingward. There was a floating TV up there. "He's odd-looking," she remarked.

"Who?"

"Well, him," she said, giving one of her familiar giggles. "Got some kind of beard on today."

"That's an icicle." I glanced up at the newsreader on the oval screen.

"Why's he want to wear an icicle, do you think?"

"He's not. The icicle's on your set, Heather. It's freezing, like everything else in this blighted place."

She giggled. "Not everything, Justy."

"Oof!" She'd given my private parts a surprise twist.

"Oh, I'm sorry, Justy. Wasn't I delicate? I want you to tell me if I'm not dainty in my caresses. Wasn't I dainty and delicate?"

"Not quite, no."

"I'm truly sorry, Justy. You know . . . Ah, now he's quite attractive."

The newsreader was holding up a tri-op color pic of a thickset blond man. "World-famous free-lance assassin Vulko McNulty is home in the shieldome of London today after another successful assignment, this time in China, Inc., where he competently and swiftly . . ."

Interesting how Vulko McNulty popped into my ken on that particular day. Right then I had no idea he'd eventually be directly involved in my life. More on that later. Forcing myself to tune out the voices from above, along with Heather's, I withdrew the food chain coupons which her part-time husband swiped from the Grub Hut where he worked as a shaper. I flipped them deftly into my nearby boot, trying to ignore the impression that ice was forming on some of my toes.

"That would be nice, wouldn't it?" inquired Heather.

"What?"

"Living in the Greater Los Angeles Citistate where it's warm the whole year round."

The newsreader was holding up a pic of a dome hotel situated amid palm trees. "The Third Annual West States Convention of the Alien Planet Welcoming Committee is being held at the Statler-Andreas Hotel in LA Citistate. Among the guests will be Bernie Kubert who, as you must know, claims to be an alien from the heretofore unknown planet of Esmeralda in a system—"

"Nutso," observed the plump Heather. "Goofy."

"Don't you believe in the possibility of life on distant planets?" Truthfully I wasn't much interested in her opinions on the possibility of extraterrestrial life, but I always tried to give her some pleasant conversation after I stole some of her Grub chits and before I slipped away from there.

"Don't tell me you do, Justy." She turned to me so rapidly her yondermost breast slapped me in the face. "Oh, I'm sorry. Did I whap you with my boopie?"

"Listen, Heather, I can put up with your calling me Justy all the time, but when you go referring to honest everyday tits as boopies it—"

"Growl!"

Wham! Bam!

"Jesus, Mary and Joseph!" Heather leaped to a standing position on the bed, pulling the inadequate quilt clean off me.

"Can that be who I suspect it is?" I nodded toward the flimsy neowood door.

"Roar! Snarl! Ugh!"

Bam! Blam!

"Yes, yes, it's my part-time husband coming home from work unexpectedly," gasped the ample girl. "And I'm afraid he sounds angry."

"He does, yes. Is he kicking something around?" I was off the bed, my backside feeling as though it were turning blue, and gathering up what clothes of mine were immediately at hand.

"He's not kicking anything, Justy. That's merely the way he climbs upstairs when he's in a bad mood."

Fortunately their apartmentette was four floors up in a liftless building. And her husband sounded a flight or more away yet. "Actually this isn't even his shift," I pointed out as I tugged on my all-season briefs and one thermal sock. "So technically he—"

"It won't make any difference," she assured me. "You've never met Umslopogaas, have you?"

"No, no, I haven't, though I've certainly heard a lot about him. But legally this isn't even his shift with—"

"Umslopogaas and I are only married for Shift 4, but when he's in one of his moods . . . He must have had more trouble in the shaping department, wherein he shapes that wonderfully nutritious Grub into various—"

"Yowl! Snarf! Rowr!"

Spam! Blang!

"He's drawing nearer," I pointed out. "Do you recall

where you tossed my shirt after you did the cooch dance with it, Heather?"

"Oh, my, no, I don't, Justy—Justin, rather. Did I mention my husband is a black man?"

"Yes, but I have nothing against colored people." I hurriedly pulled on my boots, the one with the food coupons hidden in it came first.

"He's seven feet two."

"That's tall." I checked the bed and under it, finding no trace of my shirt, all-season T-singlet or thermal greatcoat. "You didn't fling my greatcoat someplace too, did you?"

Heather was still upright on the bed, pinching her buttocks and rubbing at her stomach anxiously. "Oh, oh, oh . . . this is going to be a dreadful confrontation. You have to flee at once, Justin." She made a flapping gesture at the escape hatch which led to the roof.

"It's minus twelve degrees Celsius outside. I won't go until I locate more of—"

Thump! Rattle! Smash!

Umslopogaas, depressed apparently by some unhappy work experience at the Grub Hut, was breaking down the apartmentette door.

I went out through the hatch rapidly. This brought me out on a four-foot-wide platform four stories above the snow-filled street. I could feel the frostbite taking hold of my bare topside as I stared around. I spotted the dangling plyorope ladder which would carry me to the roof one more story up.

"Snarl! Howl!" Heather's Shift 4 husband was now inside their place, on the other side of the thin wall from me.

"Now, now, Umpsy, let me soothe your fevered brow."

"Don't understand artists, those Grub boogers," he roared. "Say my fish ain't authentic."

Listening no further, I went shinnying up the icy rope. The cold of the twilight seemed to let me alone until I got myself, flat out and panting, onto the frosted roof. Then it grabbed and I started shivering, chattering, hugging myself.

"You've pulled out of worse scrapes than this," I reminded myself. Trying to fix my features into a courageous cast, I stood up again. It didn't make me any warmer.

However, I did see now a United States Transition Service skyvan hovering some fifty yards to my right. The black and silver flying hearse, its tin angel symbol beaded with ice, was hanging between Heather's building and the one next to it.

My chief desire, considering Heather might not be able to soothe Umslopogaas' fevered brow enough if he caught sight of any of my abandoned garments, was to get off that roof and away. Rubbing my bluish hands together, taking a deep breath of spiky air, I went running across the rooftop. At the edge I sprang and caught hold of the underside landing gear of the tin angel hearse. Let me explain, if I haven't yet, I'm a tall lanky sort. Due in part to the unconventional life I've led I'm in good physical shape, damned adept at running and leaping.

So I easily caught that ice-cold metal rod and pulled myself up to the lower hatch door. I could hear, as I hung there five stories from the white street, sad music coming from an apartmentette a few feet away. Someone in there was being provided a speedy and efficient, as well as absolutely free, U.S. Government funeral.

I turned my attention from the music when I discovered the hatch was locked. My arms were feeling a bit strange, giving me the impression they might all at once decide not to function. The lock had to be circumvented quickly. This particular day, for reasons I may go into later, I wasn't carrying my laser pistol. The only alternative was to pick the damn lock while dangling from the belly of the hovering hearse by one hand.

My kit of picking tools was in my boot. Sucking in another icy inhalation of air, I let go with my left hand. My weight, which is one hundred forty pounds, suddenly felt double. Same boot as the pilfered chits. I had to, bringing my knees up like an acrobat, tug off that boot to fetch out the kit. Of course the five Grub chits came sliding out to go flapping and spinning away into the dusk.

I chose a sonicpik, managed to flick it on and press it to the lock mechanism. The lock snicked, the hatch popped open inward. I caught at the edge of the new opening with my right and then my left hand. At that point I very nearly ceased to be the subject for an autobiography. Hanging there, both arms going numb from cold and pressure, I didn't think I could haul myself all the way inside.

I hung there, hearing the nearby funeral music and deciding it was too loud and rowdy for the occasion. My brain wasn't frozen, though, and I reminded myself I was supposed to be good at things like this.

"Now do it!"

So I hauled my body over the rim, grunted and strained and did a backwards imitation of the birth ritual. Pulling the hatch shut and locking it, I stretched out flat and sighed. I was safe inside the belly of the hearse.

CHAPTER 2

The dead man they were hauling to the Nabe 13 USTS chapel was nowhere near my size, so I couldn't borrow his clothes. I traveled hunkered in the black-walled cabin of the hearse, figuring to acquire something to wear when we reached the chapel. It was somewhat warmer in the flying van, although they don't transport corpses at very high temperatures. This particular one was in his fifties, someone I remembered seeing on Heather's street a few times and possibly down at the Local, where the residents of 13 get together to complain to no avail. My mother liked to be escorted there now and then, which I did when I couldn't feign an important job interview or a Shift 4 part-time work situation. Have I mentioned that at this point in my life I was living by my wits?

You probably know, since even people in the affluent classes often have tin angel funerals, that all the flying hearses are staffed by robots. Not especially bright robots. By using a few simple tools, ones I always pack in my boots, I was able to make them think I wasn't aboard at all.

After we docked on the chapel roof, next to the sol gear, the whole hearse was lowered down a shaft to a floor two levels below the ground. I rolled out soon as the coffin compartment snapped open, not wanting to tangle with the embalming servos. Squat things with too many arms and tubes. Crouched low and still unclothed from the waist up, I dodged through the five of them rolling in for Heather's late neighbor. One of the drain troughs almost tripped me, but I maintained my balance.

With a lectrorod I'd picked up during a brief career in bashing I convinced an elevator to take me upwards to the layout floor. Most USTS funerals also give you a free wake, not to exceed fifteen minutes. Before they wheel you in for your wake you lie on your coffin cart in a big room with no windows and not much heat. I headed for there.

"Exactly right." I located a dead man in my size in the third coffin I investigated. Obviously they wouldn't put a greatcoat on him for his last journey, but he was wearing a warm-looking pullover tunic in a plaid pattern which indicated which Work Guild he'd belonged to.

Easing an arm around the guy—he was about sixty and still had bright red hair—I propped him up and tugged the pullover off. When they turn a germkill beam on certain kinds of syncloth it produces a sour odor. This tunic had it, along with a thick floral scent.

I donned it anyway and, rubbing at a corner of my eye, pushed out into a corridor to impersonate a mourner who'd lost his way.

And there was my Uncle Winsmith sniffling into his tin fist. "Justin, thank the good lord you got here," he said out of his copper throat. "Where were you? Putting the stoopis to some gumbo no doubt. But what kind of talk is that at a time like this? You ought to be ashamed, if you had any conscience which you don't, to be slipping that oversize gorkis of yours into some poor gumbo's duffy at such a sad time as this. For three days no less."

I took hold of his real arm, brought it down to his side, thinking, I guess, the gesture might turn off the flow of words from my old cyborg uncle. "I don't quite—"

"What do you ever think of save dirty things? Certainly not a regular work shift for yourself. No, all you think of is that enlarged quiffer of yours and planting it in some pootsie's poor unsuspecting—"

"Uncle Winsmith, shut up!" I suggested. "My organs are all of average size and shape. I've been out hunting for work since the last time I was home."

"Save your falsehoods, they fall on unsympathetic ears." He tapped his stainless steel ear with his tin hand. It made an annoying sound I was overly familiar with. "Me, who never had to worry about having his threadbare trousers jammed with a gargantuan boofer, who had to forgo his fair share of poot in order to toil long and hard in the Nabes for near fifty-five years. Fifty-five years spent climbing and struggling up the ladder of success."

"From Nabe 16 to Nabe 13, that's some climb."

"Can't you save the insults for a less sad time, Mr. Huge Quiffer?"

"I still don't know what you're talking about."

My uncle whacked himself across his narrow chest, producing a hollow metallic thunk. "Don't you even know your mother is dead? Don't you know we've been looking for you since yesterday? We even sent a guy from the Local over to that pootshouse where your lady friend resides with some jig with a quiffer I bet is a foot long and he broke his poor nose for him. It should have been your nose, you—"

"Damn it! Tell me what happened to my mother."

"She died. She's dead. This is her funeral. Isn't that why you're here? Or do you have another pootsie hereabouts who—"

"Dead? How can she be dead?"

"It's easy to be dead, Justin. Just merely stop living and there you are."

"Come on and tell me, you animated junkyard," I said, putting my fingers round his metal arm, "how she died?"

"I'd bet big money it was a broken heart, because she

had a son twenty years old who won't work, who always makes the Nabe Police come to the door, who—"

"Give me," I requested evenly, "the details, Uncle."

All at once he started crying, sobbing, big thick tears spilling out of his little faded eyes, splashing his wrinkled-flesh cheeks and his metal neck. "Why are we treating each other so awful at this time, Justin? I apologize. We're the only family we've got, now poor Rose is gone. What were you asking?" He wiped at his cheeks with tin fingers. "She just died, it was at work yesterday on Shift 3. Rose was only sixty and—"

"How can somebody just die? A heart attack, you mean?"

"No, it was another of her seizures, I think. She fell down, she never got up."

"Seizures? I never knew she—"

"You were never around enough to find out, to listen," my uncle accused. "It happens a lot to people who work in Plant 6. I told her to quit SeaPro, find something else. She was afraid, wanted to keep on working there so you—"

"Okay, okay. You think some of the chemicals they use to process the ocean protein for Grub had some kind of side effect?"

His head bobbed, rattling a little. "Exactly, though we'll never get SeaPro or Grub to admit it."

"Terribly sorry, Justin." Someone in a black dress and veil had come out of a parlor and into the dim corridor.

"Bothways?" I said, not certain who it was.

"I wasn't really in a girlish mood tonight," said Bothways. "You know how it is when you're an androj, some days you're girlish and some days you're boyish. The problem was, dear, the only thing black I own is this gown."

"That's okay." I moved around our downstairs neighbor and into Parlor 7. "I want to see—"

"Are you the son? I sincerely hope so." A thickset woman in a two-piece bizsuit was standing between me and the lucite platform where my mother's coffin rested.

"Yes, I'm J. C. Brinkman," I told her, believing it at the time.

She wore one of those handbag computer linkups hanging from one thick wrist. She whispered something into it, got a raspy whispered reply. "You're the only son of the late Rose Brinkman, good. Let me confirm the fact that the present whereabouts of your father is unknown. Is that correct?"

I found my fists clenching, my mouth opening and closing. I couldn't answer her right away.

"Yes, that's true," answered my uncle as he came rattling into the small brownish parlor. "Father was worse than the son, although Justin's off to a good start at beating Nate Brinkman's record. That one quiffed around the clock, never gave it a rest. Took off for good when Justin was barely three. Probably half way round the world if he hasn't blipped himself into an early—"

"Yes, fine," said the woman. "I'm Mrs-2 LaMonde, from Partz." She had a way of making her statements sound like questions, as though she wasn't exactly sure of her identity or anything else. "We prefer to wait until all the near kin have viewed the remains before collecting."

I blinked, swallowed, got my voice back. "Collecting what?"

"Your mother sold herself to Partz. I'll be taking her back to New Haven Citistate as soon as—"

"She never did that!" I glared at the woman, then at my cyborg uncle. "She didn't, did she?"

"Might be she did, to raise extra money to pay your—"

"Well, we're buying her back, Mrs. LaMonde!" I shouted.

"It's Mrs-2, since I'm only married Shifts 1 and 2," she

corrected me in a calm voice. "As to my not taking your mother's body for processing, Mr. Brinkman, I'm afraid there's no question about that. We have all the legal documents necessary, this chapel has file copies should you—"

"Listen! Nobody is going to drag off my mother's body to . . . to . . ." I took hold of one of her plump arms. "I won't let you!"

"Ah, now we can book you on a molesting charge as well."

I recognized the voice, knew when I turned I'd see Sgt-1 Lowry of the Nabe Police standing on the threshold. He held his stungun in his fist, his six-foot android partner was at his side. The andy's skin was tinted green, a favorite color of Lowry's. In its green hand it held some familiar yellow and pink arrest forms.

"My mother just died, sergeant," I said. "Can't you—"

"Figured even you'd show up at your own mom's funeral," said the cop. "Read him the charges, Biff."

"One-count-of-impersonating-an-asthmatic-to-obtain-Sudafed-illegally," read the android cop in his fluty voice. "One-count-of-selling-Sudafed-on-the-illicit-elixir-market. One-charge-of—"

"Bullshit!" I was still holding on to Mrs-2 LaMonde's fat arm. With a sudden jerk I sent her pinwheeling into the cops, real and andy.

They both tumbled over, backsides smacking the corridor flooring.

Before they hit I was charging by them. I managed to boot Lowry's stungun out of his grasp before I went running for the nearest way out.

There in the street, dappled with fresh snow, was a landcar with PARTZ emblazoned on its side. Utilizing my sonicpik, I got inside the vehicle and used my lectrorod to start it up. I was speeding away from the chapel before

Lowry or his android even reached the snow-covered street.

It wasn't until I was three blocks away from there that I realized I hadn't had a chance to take a final look at my mother.

CHAPTER 3

I didn't anticipate the Partz landcar would be locked into a preset drive pattern. Straight and true it carried me through the Nabes to the gates of the New Haven Citistate. The pickup at our Nabe 13 chapel was apparently the last one and Mrs-2 LaMonde was going to send the van home after that.

Whenever I'd been able to dodge or con my way into New Haven I always did well, almost always. The affluents are a good deal more gullible than the Nabe dwellers. I had no real objection, therefore, to being taken inside the high thick walls of the citistate. I did, though, want to avoid any further tangling with the law. I was afraid by now the vanishment of the landcar might be known to the various branches.

Back in the storage section of the rolling van were three earlier pickups, two old gentlemen plus a very large, very shaggy dog. I wondered who was going to welcome a spare part transplant from him. Probably the affluents could afford that sort of thing for their pets as well as their kin. The only empty shelf space was smack next to the dead dog, so I nudged him to one side some and stretched out. Rearranging my borrowed plaid tunic, I put on a fairly convincing semblance of death.

The Partz van, being on preset, drove itself to one of the force screen gateways in the substantial walls of New Haven, identified and awaited clearance. The profuse sweating I did during the next few moments somewhat detracted from my corpse impersonation. But word about the landcar had not as yet reached the dimwitted robots who guard the portals of the citistate. We were allowed to enter.

Since the usual cargo had little need of a view there were no windows in the rear compartment. I considered jumping out now I was safe inside the city. Then it occurred to me I might be able to unsettle some of the Partz staff. I remained prone. The van slowed, turned in somewhere and came quietly to a stop. I heard footsteps, two sets of feet at least, approaching. The rear of the van was unlocked, doors went swinging open.

After counting ten I opened my eyes and sat up on my slab. "Great news, great news!" I hollered. "There is life after death!"

Four blank eyes, two unmoving mouths. Not a gasp or an exclamation.

I hadn't anticipated—that word again—android paramedics would be doing the unloading.

"Whir click," said one of them. "Possibly not dead."

His partner suggested, "We had best report."

"I am dead, or rather I was." I hopped to the metal floor, shoved between them to jump out of the van. "What you see before you is a true and verifiable miracle. I'm off to report it to the revered Bishop of New Haven."

"Miracle? Whir click."

I glanced about me. In the middle of a plaztile courtyard is where I found myself. A low wall all around, the heavy gate we'd come through shut.

"Had we not best inform the chaplain 'bot?"

"Whir click."

Turning my plaid back on this debate, I ran at the wall. Since it was only four feet high I scaled it with no trouble. This landed me on a wide pastel blue street. I jogged along in the shadow of the elevated street ramps above, putting distance between myself and the Partz facility.

If you're not an affluent yourself you may not realize in how many small ways they live better than us. This blue plazmac street I was fleeing along, for instance. Even though a light snow was falling down through the early evening there wasn't a speck of snow underfoot nor a trace of slush. The street, like all of them in New Haven, was heated from beneath and fitted with a drain system. It made escaping much easier.

Two blocks from the Partz establishment I stopped. My intention had been to keep moving, but a large-sized man jumped into my path. He was gray-haired, wearing a very expensive two-piece synsilk offdaysuit.

"This is the house, ninny. You almost went past."

"So I did."

"I assume you feel at least a bit guilty." The large man clutched both my arms.

"A bit, yes." I had no idea who he was—he didn't appear to be law—or what he figured I ought to be guilty about. I managed, as usual in such circumstances, to feign a contrite look.

"Well, enough of this unprofitable chitchat. Come on up and fix it."

"Fix it?"

"Lad, were you not clad in the tunic of a member of the Servomech Repairmen's Guild, I'd suspect you weren't the fellow I sent for nearly two days ago."

"As a matter of fact," I confided while he guided me through a portal and onto an escalating upramp, "the man you originally summoned is dead. I'm his replacement."

My host grunted. "Where are your tools, by the way?"

"In my boot."

"An odd place to carry tools."

"It's easy to see you don't know much about guild by-laws," I told him.

"He's very droll-looking," observed a soft lazy voice from above.

Waiting for us at the ramp top was a stunning woman of thirty-one. Tall, golden-haired, clad in a plyocloth sleepsuit.

"My wife," explained the huge man, "thinks everything is droll. So much as touch her and I'll kill you on the spot."

"I doubt I'll need to touch her in the course of my work, sir."

"Very droll," said the blonde woman. "My name is Eunice, Mrs-4 Eunice Scaplan."

"We're married all four shifts," Scaplan said, tugging me out onto a third-floor balcony. "*All four.*"

"Good for you. Now where's this sick servo of yours?"

"Whoopee! Set 'em up in the next alley! Show me the way to go home! Whoopee doop!"

"There, obviously." Scaplan pointed toward the far end of the wide plazfloored balcony.

A silver-plated humanoid robot was stationed there, swaying and lurching. It held a cocktail shaker in one hand, a plazglaz in the other. A robot bartender who wasn't functioning properly.

"Yes, we've been seeing a good deal of this lately." I eased from Scaplan's grip, moved closer to the mechanism.

"Thinks it's drunk, curses like a bajtromper, can't even mix a decent syntini anymore."

"Whoops, my dear! Where's the fire? Chug-a-lug!" roared the defective robot.

"We'll have him shipshape in no time." When I removed my boot, one last Grub chit came fluttering out to land on the plaz. "Also carry my lunch in here." I shook a sonicpik into my palm.

Bonk!

The robot bartender had executed a particularly enthusiastic lurch, causing his metallic head to smack the invisible force screen which protected the balcony.

"Go away, move on!" Scaplan shouted at one of the passing private skycars. "Nothing to see!"

It was a beautiful desertgold GMFord 2-seater skycar. The kid at the controls was a good three years younger than me. Imagine owning a GMF when you're only seventeen.

"Come on over for a snort!" the robot invited. "Plenty more where this came from! Bottoms up! Spaceman's luck!"

With an angry grunt my host went inside.

"What can I mix for you, kiddo?" inquired the mechanical bartender.

"I don't drink."

"You can never have tee many syntoonis! Belly up to the bar!"

I lunged with my picklok, hit the right spot at the base of the 'bot's skull. Although National Robot & Android doesn't mention it in their ads, you can usually disable most any of their products by giving them a sonic jolt in just the proper place.

"Merry-go-round broke down," muttered the mechanism. Chin clunked against chest, it stood perfectly still now.

I studied him, thoughtful expression on my face, mumbling some trade jargon to myself. "Faulty gudgeon for sure . . . needs a new fuse link obviously . . . might as well replace the wolf tooth gearing while we're at it." Aware I'd been for the past couple minutes that Scaplan's wife was watching me through the plexidoors which separated the balcony from the living room area. I was also aware she wore three 'dustgem bracelets around her left wrist. Each one of those, fenced with the right man in Nabe 13, would bring me a thousand dollars at least. Industrial diamonds were very much in demand right then.

It never occurred to me as I stood there on that balcony with the gentle snow falling by on the other side of the force screen that I would never be back in Nabe 13 again. More about that later.

Such very small events they are which alter your life sometimes. If at that moment I'd continued to look in the direction of the watchful Eunice Scaplan instead of glancing, for no good reason, to my left all my subsequent life and adventures would have run differently.

But look to the left I did. There moving slowly through the night was a lemon yellow skycar. I didn't notice who was piloting. What I noticed was the girl sitting in the passenger seat of the softly illuminated cabin. A slim auburn-haired girl. A sensitive face, cheekbones high, a beautiful face. A face I'd last seen three years ago in a coffin. It was, there was absolutely no doubt about it, Beth.

"Beth!" I shouted. "Beth!"

She turned. She looked across at me, straight at me.

Now when you get caught looking at someone you don't know you go sort of glassy-eyed and turn away. Acting like you hadn't really been staring at all. That's what Beth tried to do that snowy evening.

She didn't quite, though, bring it off. No, for a few special seconds there was recognition in those wide green eyes of hers. She knew me and I knew her.

Then she turned away, with a slight shrug. The skycar floated off.

Forgetting Scaplan's wife and his defective robot, I poked my sonicpik into the screen control. There were a few sparks and some crackling noise before you felt the force field die. Depositing my tool in my boot, I went leaping over the balcony rail.

"Whatever are you doing, you droll young man?"

There was a walk ramp some five feet below. A fact I knew before I took my jump. Hitting it in a cannonball posture, I swiftly straightened to go running off along the outdoor ramp. Admittedly there was something of the madman about me. I had no eyes for the ramp or the people on it. All I saw was the bright yellow underside of that escaping skycar that carried Beth. Waving my arms, shouting her name, I careened along.

This wasn't the time to pause for an examination of my motives. You've no doubt realized by now I was making a fair try at living by my wits, much as Piper did. I had never, since the day I watched Beth's body go gliding through the fiery door of a tin angel cremation chamber, allowed myself to feel strongly about anyone or show much emotion over anything. Yet here I was galloping across New Haven and yowling like an idiot because I'd caught a glimpse of a girl I'd once maybe loved.

"Here now, lad!"

There was a cop running beside me now. A human cop in the scarlet and white uni of the New Haven Street Patrol. They can't carry lethal weapons, only stunguns.

"Stop thief!" I yelled.

"Thieves, is it? Where?"

"In that yellow skycar, sir." I jabbed a pointing finger at the night air. "They sniped a substantial collection of 'dustgems from my wife's boudoir."

"Isn't likely a repairman from the Nabes has a wife who can afford 'dustgems."

"Family heirlooms." Although we were both still running, the slow-moving skycar was increasing the distance between us.

"Also, son, it's not likely a gentleman with the Federal Overseers would be up to thievery."

"Federal Overseers? How do you know that, officer?"

"Because I recognize that flying vehicle. We've had special orders to look after it during its brief stay in our fair citistate." Unexpectedly he thrust a foot in front of mine.

We both tripped and I went tumbling and sliding along the heated ramp. I got up, found myself in the midst of a group of well-dressed affluents who were crossing toward a palatial town house. The SP cop was having a difficult time arising. Did I mention I'd managed to knee him in the groin before I disentangled myself?

I mingled with the guests, entered the house with them. Anxious as I was to pursue Beth, I knew I didn't want to get arrested. An attractive, though nearly forty, red-haired woman in an off-the-bosom synlon partisuit, was next to me.

"Surely Mona didn't invite a handyman to the wedding?" she said, frowning.

I gave her a chuckle. "Wouldn't you know it, lady," I said with faultless low Nabe inflections. "The nerfing bath robot went kaflooey. Got to repair it right away else there's trouble for one and all."

"Is that what your tartan indicates? That you repair servos? I can never tell one working class plaid from another." She brushed a few flecks of melting snow off one of her handsome breasts.

I hate to admit it, but at a time when I should have been thinking of the sad passing of my mother and the miraculous return of Beth I watched that affluent lady's breast with considerable attentiveness. "No reason you should, ma'am."

"You're quite youthful," she said, speaking close to my

ear, "and quite handsome, if you don't mind my saying so, for a repairperson."

"Actually I'm only an apprentice."

"I told you we'd be late, Danni." A pudgy man took the redhead's hand. "Look, they're already coming down the aisle."

We were milling in the vast domed foyer. In a circular room beyond, a hundred people were rising to their feet as a giant ivory-paneled automatorgan commenced playing a wedding march. Waddling down the aisle between the licorice-hued chairs was a very old and fat woman. She wore a peach-color off-the-bosom bridesuit.

When I saw who was waiting at the altar beside the All-denom minister I couldn't help making a noise like Scaplan's malfunctioning robot. "Whoops!" I exclaimed aloud.

Standing there, about to be a groom, was Piper.

CHAPTER 4

Piper I'd first met in the Chicago Citistate Nabes when I was scarcely seventeen. A tall man, wide and swarthy, a few months beyond thirty and one of the best confidence men and all-around rogues I'd ever encountered. He'd allowed me, sensing my larcenous streak and other native abilities, to help out on a few of his ventures. I hadn't seen him in over a year or more.

Here he was at the altar, dressed exactly right in a two-piece neosilk weddingsuit of midnight blue. On his tanned face, immediately below his smartly clipped moustache, was a smile. Having known and worked with him I immediately recognized that smile as the one he called Pious #3. So I realized, once my surprise at encountering him here had let go my thinking equipment, exactly what he had in mind for that unappealing old bimbo.

There was some scuffling behind me, a bit of low muttering. I sensed, without risking a glance around, the street cop was up and around and searching for me. Close by was a rampway, which I decided to avail myself of.

"Must you?"

I became aware the redhead had hold of one of my hands. "We can't have a malfunctioning chef 'bot on a day like this, lady." I disengaged myself.

"Didn't you say it was the crapper that was on the fritz?"

"In reality it's both, ma'am. Never rains but it pours, as

we say in the Nabes." I touched my forehead with a respectful finger and, keeping as many people as possible between me and the questing cop, went sprinting up the ramp and through an arched doorway.

Two husky men and a robot raised guns to point at me. Not stun weapons, but the considerably more unsettling laser types. "Blow off," advised one of the humans.

The pastel pink room was crammed with magnificently wrapped wedding gifts. They overflowed the three floating lucite tables, were piled on the see-through floor, even jammed into several of the lycra slingchairs. The robot, who was seated on an aluminum sofa, even had a few gifts piled on his metal lap.

I shook my head, smiling in a puzzled way. Guileless #4, that was what Piper had called it when he taught me the whole repertoire. "These big houses sure can confuse a guy," I said. "Could one of you gentlemen show me to the bathroom?"

"You can't go taking a weep during the frigging ceremony," the big private cop who'd spoken earlier informed me.

"Right, I know. But what I'm here to do is patch up the whirlpool in the john."

From out a speaker in the curving ceiling came the wedding ceremony. "Do you, Angelo Otranto of Profane Rome, take this . . ."

Piper was apparently doing his Italian nobleman.

"You can see by my attire," I continued, "that I'm a bonafide repairperson."

"Trousers." The other live guard aimed his laser pistol at an essential part of my person.

"How's that, sir?"

"Never saw a reep in fancy pants like those."

I chuckled, nodded, let him have a shot of Confidential Smile #2, also known as just-between-us-fellows. "You know, I told my two-shift idiot of a wife the same darn thing. Right before I departed our Nabe to whiz over here to serve my betters. 'Where about are my work trousers?' 'Never came back out of the laundry chute,' I am informed. 'Never came back?' 'Isn't that what I'm telling you,' she says, 'and you a repairman. Why don't you fix this dump of an–' "

"Go on to the bathroom. It's over that way." The robot jerked a metal thumb toward a pale green door. "I want to hear the wedding. They always break me up."

"He's programmed that way," said a human guard. "They make special kinds of 'bots for weddings and funerals and other such sentimental occasions. See, he's crying."

"Oh, then those are tears." I hastened to the door. "I thought he might be leaking. Still, if he ever does need fixing, my name is–"

"Out, depart," said the sad robot.

From the speaker I caught Piper's voice declaring, "I most certainly do."

Seeing Beth again, for all the impact it had on me, hadn't done much in the way of reforming me. I have to acknowledge that as I pushed into the long persimmon-color corridor my chief regret was not being able to grab off a few of those gifts.

The corridor wound and climbed and I finally arrived at a pair of ivory white doors trimmed with what had to be real gold. It was a matter of only a minute or so to fetch an electroscrewer from out my boot and apply it to one of the gleaming golden door handles. Had to be worth at least six hundred from any pawner in Nabe 13.

"Help. Oh, my. What the . . . ooof." Very faintly from the other side of the white doors a feeble voice had sounded.

Next came a thud, suggesting a heavyset woman had

fallen to the floor, landing on an expensive thermal carpet.

Replacing the gold door handle swiftly, I opened the door of the bath suite.

A long, warm and floral-scented alley of white and gold stretched away from the opening. Farther off, across the immense white plazflooring, a half-open door showed me an enormous bedchamber. That room was all rose and pink, softly illumed by a good dozen floating, lace-trimmed globes of pale pinkish light.

Kneeling on the thick pink rug was Piper. He was in the process of stuffing his recent bride into a rose-colored plyosack. Her hands and feet were already taped and Piper was applying the final turn of thick tape across her mouth.

After he nudged the entire bulk of his hefty bride, effortlessly, into the sack, Piper arose and grinned at me.

Possibly it was Disarming Grin #1, possibly it was real. I chose to interpret it as authentic. I shut the bath suite door behind me and eased into the rosy bedchamber. "Working the spurious marriage dodge again, huh?"

"Trot over to yonder closet, my boy, and deck yourself out in one of the little woman's frocks," he suggested.

"Haven't run into you since we—"

"Justin, you have to get rid of the unfortunate habit of putting personal feelings ahead of the business at hand." Using one booted foot, he rolled his sacked bride under her large floating bed. "With you suitably attired, we can bluff out the main exit and save the time and effort of climbing down the side of this joint."

"The preacher's in it with you?"

"Did he strike you as completely plausible?" Piper was at a vanity console, using a leckey on various drawers. "While I gather up the $200,000 in 'dustgems and real-pearls, you try to transform yourself into a fairly reasonable replica of the missus."

"She's awfully fat." Slowly I was making my way to the wide closet he'd indicated.

"Who knows better than I, my boy. You little realize what I've had to wrestle with in order to get possession of this key today." He was scooping handfuls of gems into a synlap satchel that had *Just Wed!* scrawled on its nubby side in red. "She insisted on taking the uppermost position in every blessed sexual bout we had. If you've ever had a two hundred and seventy-four-pound lass pounce gleefully upon you, Justin, then you can—"

"We're going to do the surprise honeymoon getaway?"

"Has it ever failed me?"

"According to what you told me, once in the Memphis Redoubt, with spectacular res—"

"We are not, you'll notice, anywhere near Memphis." Piper paused to fluff his moustache before returning to packing baubles. "When I carry you, romantically, out the front portals of this place, the entire crowd of dim-witted affluents will be too awed to do anything but sigh."

"Who wouldn't be awed, seeing a guy heft a three-hundred-pound old squack."

Piper grinned. "Justin, if you do a thing with enough flair and style, not one mark in a thousand will ever stop to ponder upon it. Trust me."

I was, with considerable reluctance, getting into a sky-blue daysuit of the old woman's. I don't like cons that require any drag work. "This is going to need a lot of padding."

"Use the bedding, since I don't need it to construct a rope anymore."

"How've you been?"

"You still have, despite all the effort I've put into the

task, a lot to learn about the priorities in life and the true—"

"How's the padding in front? Enough?"

"No, she's considerably more saggy around the yonkers, as who knows better than your humble servant. Add that bolster, my boy." He scanned the room, nodded, and shut up the satchel. "I was lecturing you on something of vital importance, wasn't I?"

"The meaning of life." I'd discovered a whole shelf of the stashed-away bride's wigs. Each a different color and texture, each perched on a huge plaz egg. I selected one that seemed especially festive and plopped it, none too carefully, on my head.

He was scrutinizing me, one gray eye narrowed, knuckle rubbing at his prominent jaw. "Ah, you've achieved just the right tacky effect." Bending from the waist, he snatched up the old lady's fallen bridal veil and tossed it to me. "Drape this over your skonce and we'll fool the whole pack of 'em. As to the meaning of life, there is none."

"I suspected as much."

"Bride and groom!"

"Happy pair!"

"What's afoot?"

Considerable shouting, laughing and chanting were drifting up from below.

Piper crossed to the door, urged it open with his knee. "I doubt any of these louts will get a good gander at you inside that netting but, just in case, you better keep Ecstatic #5 frozen on your puss. Okay?"

I walked over to him and Piper scooped me up and carried me down a corridor and down a ramp bride-fashion. We were soon surrounded by wedding guests.

"Here they are!"

"Doesn't Mona look wonderful!"

"And he's so handsome, for an Italian."

"Oh, not now, officer."

I noted, through my gauzy face covering, that the street cop was still moving through the group, peering into faces and attempting a little moderate frisking.

"Joyful Sigh #6," whispered Piper as we neared the open doorway.

I sighed appropriately and we were across the threshold and heading for a hovering skycar.

When we were climbing away above the bright-lit rooftops of New Haven, I got very rapidly out of my disguise. "Things have been changing for me," I said across to Piper.

He was in the drive seat. "Don't tell me you really are a repairman?"

"No, I'm still living by my wits."

"The only course open to such as us."

"My mother died yesterday."

His real face emerged for a few seconds. "I'm sorry, she was a good person."

I realized something. "There's no real need for me to go back to Nabe 13 at all."

"My immediate plans call for leaving New Haven and environs far behind," Piper said. "There are a few interesting enterprises down in the Rio Enclave I'm anxious to investigate. Why not come along?"

I shook my head, telling him, "Listen, Piper, I saw Beth Danner today, right here inside the walls of New Haven."

"Beth Danner, the lass you were so taken with in Chicago?" He frowned. "She's dead and gone, Justin. I was there when they consigned her to the flames, as were you."

"I know that, Piper. Except, honest to god, I saw her tonight."

"How many times have we made some nitwit see anything we wanted him to see?" Piper was heading the borrowed skycar across the dark waters of the Sound. "You possess, and I've struggled vainly to purge you of it, a strong sentimental streak. The girl is dead and you should have ceased mooning over her years ago. Instead you con yourself, the worst sin there is, by the way, into thinking you've actually spotted her alive and kicking. What did she say when you approached her?"

"Well, nothing, actually. See, she . . ." I recounted to him everything that had happened since I took leave of Heather.

Then Piper laughed. "You should have dallied with Scaplan's dissatisfied wife. You'd be a bracelet or two to the good now."

"Damn it, it was Beth," I told him. "I've got a good eye, Piper, you know that. They can't fool me, not about something like this."

He knuckled his moustache. "You do have a pretty fair eye at that," he said thoughtfully. "Except I don't see how the hell Beth can possibly be alive."

"But she is."

"We will, my boy, have to look into this."

"Yeah, and the place to start is New Haven Citistate," I reminded him. "You don't want to go back there right now, do you?"

"Be that as it may, we'll have to look into this," Piper said.

CHAPTER 5

Another black Rabbi came climbing over the mounds of rubble. Not quite seven feet tall this one, making him the runt of the pack, and decked out in the now familiar dark greatcoat, black skullcap and chest-length false whiskers. He held an acidpistol, too, just like the other six Negro rabbis who were stalking through the piles of snow-crusted brick and rusted iron toward us.

"Good evening, gents," said Piper, slowing. "Always uplifting to encounter some gentlemen of the cloth."

"This here the 2400 block, hump," pointed out the tallest black young man.

"Exactly," agreed Piper, sharing an Undaunted Grin #2 with them all. "Once I've stashed my skycar in a safe hideaway, I always find this route best for arriving at the 2300 block."

They drifted closer to us, as quiet as the softly falling night snow, acid-spitting pistols aimed. "2400 block, 'cording to the Brooklyn Depths Treaty of 2029, hump-stick, belongs exclusive to the Vicious Black Rabbis," explained the leader. "Namely that is us."

Piper inquired, "What happened to Joshua?"

"The Crazed Rican Arch Bishops killed him off way last month."

"Sorry to hear that." Piper made himself look sad for a few seconds.

"Killed him and barbecued him," the Rabbi leader

elaborated. "You could smell him cooking for blocks around."

"Them dirty humps sprinkle lotsa oregano all over him," added another of the black gang members. "Plus they own special blend of hot sauce."

"A touching and terrible way to go." Piper nodded glumly. "Joshua and I had an agreement. I'm Piper."

"Piper?" The leader lowered his gun, stroked his fake beard. "I heard of you, but never thought to meet you. You a legend, humper."

"In my own time, yes," admitted Piper, grinning, moustache perking. "This is my close friend and comrade, Justin Brinkman. We're en route to the 2300 block to pay a social call on another longtime chum of mine, Taplinger."

"Mama's boy," observed a Rabbi.

"A gifted info siphoner nonetheless." Piper urged me onward by taking my elbow and increasing his pace. "Well, good evening, one and all."

"Nice meeting you," said the leader.

When we were a half block from them, I asked, "They actually practice cannibalism in Brooklyn Depths?"

"There isn't anything they don't practice in Brooklyn."

We crossed a street, arrived at a block where almost half the buildings were still intact. Across the way, in the shell of a dead hardware store, you could see a cook fire flickering.

Piper, after sniffing at the air, said, "Cat meat."

"Glad to hear that."

Up ahead of us a one-armed old man in a tattered Universal Army overcoat was climbing his way up a rickety ladder to change a dim electric sign. In his only hand he clutched a square of plaz with the number 1026 painted on it.

Junior Miss Bordello was the place's name. The old guy was going to insert the new number in the part of the sign which read: *Over 1025 Underage Virgins Ruined to Date!*

"A nasty business," I remarked.

"Unimpressive profit margin, too." Piper nodded at a narrow, leaning shop with *Mom & Pop's Grocerette* scribbled across its dusty window in nonfunctioning neon tubing. "Our destination, my boy."

"You sure this Taplinger can help us? Seems to me heading right back to New Haven would be a—"

"Trust me," suggested Piper, knocking on the store's faded real wood door. "This is by far the safest, and most efficient way."

"Yeah, but Beth is over there and we—"

"Patience," said Piper. "There's another knack I'd like to see you pick up."

Something meowed just on the other side of the door.

"Would that be Piper?" asked a thin voice.

"None other."

Nothing happened with the door.

"You absolutely guarantee me it's you, Piper?" said the thin-voiced man.

"The genuine article, Taplinger. Now let us in, there are a lot of cannibals roaming your neighborhood tonight."

Locks whirred, hummed, rattled. "Not bad enough they eat each other, they been getting our cats as well." Taplinger's pale little face showed in the six-inch opening. "Ever smelled a dear pet of yours being fricasseed over an open fire?"

"Sounds cozy." Piper pushed the door all the way open and we went in.

Taplinger was exactly five feet tall. Dressed in a flannel bathrobe over a two-piece tan worksuit. He was barefooted and had too many toes. Seven on the right foot at least.

"Eight on the right, nine on the left," he said to me,

sensing what I was doing. "They used to dump some kind of strange chemical waste nearby some years back. Caused a lot of mutations."

A three-eyed cat came up and purred around my ankle.

Piper glanced around the room. "How's your dear mother?"

All of the grocery shelves were empty and dusty. At one side of the small room sat what looked to be a computer terminal, except it had all sorts of gimcrack additions—pieces of plaz tubing, old-fashioned lightbulbs, a twisted metal coat hanger, part of a vidrecorder, the insides of at least two digital clocks, and quite a few bits of wire, tubing and plaz I couldn't identify at all.

"The old hag?" Taplinger went shuffling toward his modified computer terminal. "I think, praise be, she's finally dying."

"A shame," said Piper, shooing a five-legged cat off a lopsided chair and sitting.

"Thought for sure the old bat would kick off last winter, after she broke her dang hip. That was while she was running from the Ruin Cops. Leaped between two tenements, whipped down a drainpipe and then fell into a manhole."

Piper said, "An admirable old person, plucky and unsinkable."

"A pain in the took, if you'll pardon my French." Taplinger hunched, squinted at his computer rig. "Damn and hell, one of the cats did his business on this. Fix it in a sec, excuse me, fellows."

He shuffled out through a curtained doorway, followed by the three-eyed cat, the five-legged cat and a greenish one with an extra tail.

"Listen." I moved closer to my seated friend. "This guy doesn't inspire confidence."

"Don't let a few personality flaws cloud your judgment, my boy."

"Yow!" cried someone in another room.

I straightened up. "What's that?"

"Little harmless roughhousing twixt Tap and his mom."

"Hell, that was a scream of pain."

"Mrs. Taplinger is a very feisty old lady."

Taplinger was limping when he returned, carrying a portavac in his hands. "Ever have a hot water bottle uncorked and then upended over your fanny, pardon my Dutch?" The back of his robe had a large dark blotch on it.

While he was vacuuming the computer terminal, Piper said, "We wish to consult some U. S. Government files, Tap."

"Rich widow of a deceased colonel maybe?" asked Taplinger, chuckling. "Those old broads get a darn substantial pension from—"

"The information is, mostly, for my young friend, Justin."

Taplinger turned to study me. "Mother living?"

"Just died."

"Boy, what I wouldn't give for a break like— Did you hear a thump?"

"No."

"Guess not." He sighed. "Was hoping the old bag had fallen out of bed and broken something else. No such luck."

"You can siphon the files of the Federal Overseers, can't you?" Piper left his chair, stepped across a sleeping earless cat and went over to where Taplinger was tinkering.

He made a pained face. "FO? That's risky, Pipe."

"Which is why, dear pal, we'll pay extra."

"Well, there's nothing I can't patch into." Taplinger chuckled. "Mother has a very low opinion of me, but I am a brilliant fellow. Conceived and built this little gem you– Was that a groan?"

"Nope," I said.

"Any idea what the death rattle sounds like? Be helpful to know, that way when she starts producing one I'll be ready for–"

"We want to find out about a yellow FO skycruiser that was over in the New Haven Citistate this afternoon," Piper told him.

"New Haven, there's where I'd love to settle down some fine day," said Taplinger, eyes nearly shut. "Once the old battleax croaks, I'm going to sell my invention for a tidy sum and buy a little nest in some spot like New Haven, or maybe a warmer one. Might even marry, since fifty-three isn't too old for that sort of activity."

"Not at all," said Piper. "Though I'd be most careful about unloading your unique mechanism, Tap. Before you do, let me give you some helpful hints on how to turn your present situation into a much more lucrative one."

"Go ahead, tell me."

"Unfortunately, we're working against a tight deadline just now." Piper gave him one of his best Ruefuls. "As soon as our mission is completed, though, I'll pop back here."

"Really appreciate that," said Taplinger. "The old battleax thinks I'll never earn more than $100,000 per. Heck beck, a fellow with my brain setup might even own New Haven some sweet day. Soon as I get her planted in the sod, I–"

"Federal Overseers," reminded Piper, placing a broad hand on the small man's flanneled back.

The ramshackle bentwood chair Taplinger dragged over made a shrill keening sound on the slaty flooring. He seated himself in front of the terminal, spit on his palms and rubbed them vigorously together. He started poking buttons, turning dials, yanking on dangles of wire and twists of tubing.

After some thirty seconds of this the computer's voxbox coughed and, in a voice amazingly like Taplinger's, said, "Clarenson, Elizabeth, Agent Special Class. Oxner, Bram, Agent First Class."

Piper glanced across at me. "That's who was riding in your cruiser, my boy."

I went over to them. "Could be more than one skycar was—"

"Naw," Taplinger assured me, "this is the only one anywhere near there today."

"The first name is right," I said. "She could have changed her last one. Piper, I *know* it was Beth."

"Get us some background on the lass," Piper requested.

Hunching, spitting afresh, Taplinger poked, probed, twisted.

"Urp urp," spoke the computer after more than a minute.

Taplinger jumped to his feet, yanked at a switch on the wall and then unplugged three short red and yellow wires. "I'll be damned, if you'll pardon my Chinese," he said, letting out a sigh.

"Trouble?" asked Piper.

"When I tried to go back any further than two years into this girl's BG, we hit a blox circuit."

"That's an extra precaution they rarely take, mainly because it's expensive." Piper smoothed his moustache, left side and then right side. "Reserve it for very important stuff and people."

Taplinger gave a cautious shrug. "Is she?"

Piper frowned at me. "To us, yes," he replied slowly.

"To our esteemed government, I wouldn't have thought so."

"I can maybe work around their block," offered Taplinger. "Going to take a day or more, though, and I'll probably have to modify the machine slightly."

"First find out what the girl was doing in New Haven," said Piper. "Then where she's going from there."

"Oh, that'll be a snap," promised Taplinger.

CHAPTER 6

It was warm. Inside of course, but also, more importantly, outside. The day was clear and bright and beyond the see-through walls of the highup floating bubble restaurant the capital city of Ereguay was shining in the midday sunlight. Its buildings were mostly white, with gleaming red plaztile roofs. The bay, known locally as Baía Beleza, was immense and a crystal blue. The imitation palms lining the wide mosaicked streets looked hazy green and absolutely real from up at our restaurant table.

"Not even one deadly missile?" asked the nervous blond man Piper and I were lunching with.

"Nary a one, Stacy." Piper sipped his double syntini.

Stacy Towers rubbed his hands along the legs of his off-white funsuit trousers. "I expected most of the Eastern Seaboard would be in absolute and total ruin by now."

"You've heard about that on the news."

"The news is all managed and spruced up down here."

Piper burnished some of the brass buttons on his blue tunic with his plyonap. "Could well be, Stacy, you went into hiding too soon."

"Wouldn't you know it," he said, grimacing. "That's what I get for trusting a Sears home computer. Damn thing swore up and down there'd be a devastating atomic attack on the entire East Coast no later than 2033. When I read that off the display screen, I bundled up Roscoe and the kids . . . Homosexual marriages don't bother you, do they, Justin?"

"They're fine for other folks," I said.

"Been rough on the kids down here," Towers said. "Been rough on all of us, in fact. Imagine living in a country where they speak nothing but Portuguese, day in and day out. Christ."

"Why'd you pick Ereguay to escape doom in, old chum?"

"I didn't, it was that damn Sears home computer again. Safest country in the whole round world in the event of a ruthless missile strike on the West by certain red-oriented nations." He gazed out at the Baía. "You suppose that frigging thing just needed a tuneup? Maybe I shouldn't have panicked, especially when Roscoe's day care center was really starting to perk up."

Out on a low mountain beside the bay stood a several-story-high piece of sculpture. It showed Christ getting a hand with his cross from Saint Avaro. You don't hear much about Avaro these days, but the capital of this newest South American country was named after him.

". . . attractive."

I turned. Apparently Towers had been addressing me. "Beg pardon?"

"I was commenting on how very attractive you look in your Child Salvation Corps uniform, although it's a bit tight across the buttocks."

"Thanks." Apparently I recoiled slightly at his compliment.

"Don't be afraid, Justin," he said, smiling, "I'm a happily married man."

"We appreciate your arranging these outfits for us, Stacy," said Piper. "They provide us a splendid cover for roaming São Avaro and environs."

They also tied in with some black market scheme Piper wanted to explore while we were down here. It had something to do with diverting a couple of skyvan loads of basic Grub and I was hoping I wouldn't get involved at all. Towers worked for the CSC, though not in uniform, and he was going to have something to do with Piper's notion, too.

"What about," I put in, "Beth Danner?"

"Better known as little Liz Clarenson." Piper leaned an elbow on the oval glaz tabletop. "What have you come up with, Stacy?"

Towers scanned the room. The place wasn't crowded. Less than twenty other people were sharing the place with us. "I contacted my contact and . . ."

"And?" prompted Piper after a spell of silence.

Towers switched to whispering. I missed what he said next.

I inched my plaz chair nearer to him. "Huh?"

"He says the girl is definitely in Ereguay," Piper interpreted.

"Not so loud," warned Towers.

"Taplinger's half-ass computer gave us that much, which is why we're here," I said, letting my impatience and disappointment show. "We want to know exactly where she is now. We need specifics."

"Where is she?" Piper asked him. "What's she doing?"

Towers shook his head, licked at his upper lip, returned to staring at the bright blue bay. "This could well be something none of us wants to fiddle with."

"Pretend you're a simple computer terminal, dear pal." Piper put a hand on his arm and applied pressure. "Simply provide us the bald, bare-assed facts. Let us worry about the repercussions."

When he faced us again, Towers' face was dotted with sweat. "Do you know who Jorge Beijar is?"

"He's leader of the guerrillas who're fighting against the present dictatorship," I responded.

"Don't holler it out."

"Didn't."

Towers inhaled, exhaled, inhaled. All slowly. "She, this girl, is down here on a very delicate Federal Overseers mission, one they most certainly don't want publicized," he said, voice very low. "She and her partner, the Oxner guy, picked up someone in New Haven and escorted him here."

After another sip of his drink, Piper asked, "Who'd they haul South?"

"Mumble mumble."

"Raise the volume a few notches, old pal."

"His name is Dozer, Dr. Leo Dozer."

Piper laughed. "Not *the* Dr. Dozer, father of the Dozerizer?"

"Him, yes. Don't go hooting his name so openly," said Towers, tongue sliding across his upper lip. "Lots of the military people in Ereguay swear by the Dozerizer."

"What is the thing?" I imagined we were talking about some kind of household appliance and was trying to figure how its inventor was going to aid the Ereguayan dictatorship against the Beijar-led rebels who were shooting up the provinces to the north of the capital.

"Little gadget for attaching to your privatemost parts," Piper explained. "Had the pleasure of having one attached to me in White Mississippi some years ago by a local tycoon who was extremely curious as to the whereabouts of his young and fetching second wife and three skyvans full of his finest-grade moonshine."

"A torture device?"

"To say the least." Piper winced at the recollection. "Do you know, I had to refrain from dipping the old kazoo for—"

"Easy now," cautioned Towers. "A real Salvation lieutenant doesn't talk about dipping any—"

"You're absolutely right. I've got to match my lingo to

my façade," Piper said. "What exactly did the Clarenson girl bring the good doctor here for?"

"They've got Jorge Beijar's youngest sister, captured her last week," continued Towers in a low voice. "Word is Dr. Dozer has a new, more compact inquiry device. He's apparently agreed to use it on the girl. That's the reason the FO agents escorted him here."

"How old's the lass?"

"Nineteen next month."

"Hell, Beth wouldn't do anything like that," I said, angry. "I've known her for–"

"We're not dealing with Beth Danner, my boy, we're dealing with Special Agent Clarenson."

"You don't know her," I insisted. "Are you trying to tell me, again, that I'm goofy? I tell you I did see–"

"Justin, m'lad, I believe you saw Beth alive." He looked directly at me, left eye narrowing. "I also believe we're on the brink of discovering something important, and quite possibly lucrative. Thus far we've only sighted the tip of this particular mountain. A very strong hunch keeps banging around inside my coco, has been ever since you and I were reunited on the fateful eve of my nuptials. What I think–"

"Are you married, Piper? Congratulations." Towers brightened. "Many people knock the institution these days, even Roscoe shows an occasional flash of scorn, but let me assure you that marriage is the–"

"This was not exactly a genuine and completely authentic wedding," Piper told him. "Spurious marriages are one of the occupational hazards I face in my line of work. This latest pseudo bride, I must admit, looked better inside a plyosack than– But I was about to impart something significant to you, Justin."

"You were rationalizing our jaunt down here to South America."

"I don't claim, as some of my cronies both here and on the Continent, to possess much in the way of extrasensory powers." He perked his moustache with a forefinger. "However, I feel we're embarked on an important task. We had been going along fully convinced, for long sad years, that the lass was dead and gone. Indeed, that she was long since no more than a small, gritty mound of ashes. Now we discover she's far from that and is instead a full-fledged agent for our own proud and democratic land. Damn it, my boy, there's something strange going on."

"Don't fool with it," advised Towers. "Piper, this deal you and I are contemplating. It'll garner at least a million five for us. I'm talking net, not gross. Half of that sum is—"

"Sixty percent is nine hundred thousand," put in Piper, "the exact sum I'll require for participating."

"Sixty? Come on, you know damn well I can get a local operator to—"

"Ah, but he'd no doubt speak only Portuguese," reminded Piper. "Whereas, while proficient in that tongue, I offer you flawless schoolmarm English and several varieties of vernacular street American."

"Okay, sixty. But don't tell Roscoe."

"If my life runs as anticipated, I'll not so much as set eyes on your mate this time around."

"Did you find out anything more about her?" I asked Towers. So far we didn't know all that much more than we had when we left Taplinger's Brooklyn Depths hideaway two days before. His computer siphon had already told us where Beth was going. That was why we were in the heart of Ereguay, dressed in uniforms and pretending to be interested in war orphans and their rehabilitation. "Is she in São Avaro or some other town?"

"Not sure, Justin. I should know more in a day or so,"

Towers said. "Right now, Piper, you and I have some other important things to talk over."

Pushing back from the table, I said, "I'll stroll back to our hotel."

"Remember to look as benevolent as you can, my boy."

Which is why I still had a beatific smirk on my face ten minutes later when none other than Twilight Malone herself came rocketing into my life.

CHAPTER 7

That afternoon I met her she was the top-rated woman in the Western Hemisphere. Her midnight newscast on Sat-Net-1 was the most watched television show in both North and South America and her dawncast, *Intimate News,* was changing the viewing habits of all fifty-three states and pulling viewers, especially guys, up at a very ungodly hour. Twilight Malone was twenty-six, a little less than five feet eleven, black and absolutely lovely. Once you watched her midnight news broadcast, saw her sprawling on that pink neosilk bed in her frilly negligee, you became a current events fan. Your interest in world affairs increased amazingly, you wanted Twilight Malone to fill you in on war, famine, pestilence, death and the weather. And her morning show, with her in a bubble bath Mondays and Wednesdays and a shower the rest of the week, contained the most provocative political commentary ever aired. The National Academy of Video Artists had recently awarded her a gold cup saying just that.

I encountered Twilight because her silver landcar happened to go berserk at exactly the moment I was strolling along the Avenue of the Benevolent Despots.

The clear blue São Avaro sky was dotted with uniformed men, fifteen or twenty of them in snappy black and gold outfits. They were using skybelts, zooming down out of a high, hovering Polícia Federal skyvan. Their objective was a shop with the ill-chosen name of the Liberal Minded Book Emporium.

The diving cops were shooting disabler rays and stunbeams into the place, blasting away at the live help and the robot equipment. Armor-suited patrolmen were stomping around inside the place, smashing servos, printboxes, and display shelving. One of the damaged faxprinters was making a gobbling noise while it spewed six-color comic pages of graphic versions of the classics out into the early afternoon street.

I stopped short of the shop, bent to pull a bright page of *Swann's Way* off my boot heel. Then's when I noticed Twilight.

Across the street she was, dashing out of a Grub Hut with one of their familiar yellow Grub Buckets full of imitation food clutched to her handsome chest. "Futz off, you clunkorooneys," she was advising a cluster of her fans. "Watch the flapping riot or something."

I'd never seen her with her clothes on before. She was really stunning, her long red hair flashing, the silky black skin on her fascinating face highlighted with one subtle silver beauty patch in the shape of a Maltese cross.

She moved with admirable grace, even when she sidearmed an overzealous Ereguayan lad aside and caused him and his autograph pad to go spinning.

"Heed your public, hussy!" warned an old woman in a plyoshawl, the glaz rosary beads in her gnarled hand quivering and clicking.

"Up your snootorooney, granny!" Twilight shoved her way into her car with her load of Grub, locked all the doors, and activated the Shockem System.

The silver vehicle began to sizzle all along its gleaming surface. Those fans who'd been trying to climb on it commenced howling with pain and surprise. As they fell to the street, Twilight went gunning away from the curb.

She executed a screeching U-turn and came whizzing in my direction.

A tardy Fed was zipping down through the afternoon and his stungun went off prematurely, sending a bolt of force slamming into the hood of Twilight's landcar.

Immediately thereafter the car said, "Pock!" Greenish vapor came swirling from beneath the lid of the elecengine.

I could see the stunning black girl pounding at the control panel with angry fists. The car kept saying, "Pock! Pock!" It went into a circling pattern, roaring around and around in neat circles, spitting out more green smoke.

"Serves her right, the hussy!"

I hopped onto one foot, yanked off my boot and snatched out my sonicpik. Swiftly tugging the boot back on, and then dodging the wedge of cops who were dragging the protesting shopkeeper out of his place, I ran into the street.

Several slippery pages of the middle section of *The Anatomy of Melancholy* nearly made me trip. I managed to hold my balance and get into the street.

Twilight was fighting with the dash panel, screaming at it.

The car, though, was entirely out of her control, wildly malfunctioning and inscribing circles on the picturesque plaz cobblestones.

I watched it make another full circle run before I leaped onto the front hood. She still had the damn Shockem activated, causing my body to jerk and my teeth to grit. Even so I held on, successfully thrusting the pik into that little hole just to the left of the frontal scanner. GMFord doesn't circulate the fact widely, but you can nearly always disable one of their landcars by doing that. Deftly enough.

The vehicle sighed, broke out of its circular rut to go bucketing across the wide street. It climbed the curb, bonged into the bole of an imitation palm tree.

The immutable laws of nature being what they are, I continued to move. Sailing free of the hood, I flew smack into the unyielding plaz window of the Grub Hut that Twilight had recently visited.

I hit that window very damn hard and everything went away from me.

Surrounded by images. They climbed up the walls all around my bed. Video monitor screens, each one a good two feet wide, showing me what was going on in the world. There was Vulko McNulty, very dapper in a three-piece lime funsuit, kilgun resting casually on his knee as he sat in a familiar Grub Hut booth. There was no sound accompanying any of the many pictures, but I was pretty good at reading lips, a knack Piper taught me the time we worked one of his dodges at a dog track in Pittsburgh Enclave.

". . . a place you can really relax," the celebrated assassin was silently saying, blond hair slicked back off his low, furrowed forehead. "And that means a Grub Hut. It's really comforting to know, believe you me, no matter where my work takes me, that I'm going to find Grub. Grub's the best, and we'll send you the lab results to back this up in case your very own taste buds haven't already confirmed the fact, the best-tasting synfood on this weary old globe of . . ."

And there, two screens up and one over, was the President of the United States, Wildman Woolinsky. He was a big, wide, affable man, dressed in one of those two-piece overall suits which had done so much to win him the election. This was some sort of outdoor press conference, upwards of a hundred reporters were squatting around on the sand in front of the Alternate White House in Taos, New Mexico.

". . . repeat that for the benefit of the Washington

Post-Star," Wildman Woolinsky was mouthing. "I gave up all connection with my used car dealerships when I assumed office."

"Then why, Mr. President, are there price tags on all the cars parked in your drive?"

"Aw, Mr. Reisberson, that's only the Secret Service boys having some fun."

"Is it true, Mr. President, you had a long and leisurely luncheon last week with Bernie Kubert, the self-styled off-planet alien, at a Washington, D.C., Grub Hut?"

"I did. Bernie's a very intelligent and articulate fellow," said the President. "I think if all aliens are as perceptive and well-mannered as he is, why, we'll get along just fine when an alien armada happens to land here from some hitherto unheard of planet."

"Are you implying, Mr. President, you have some information predicting such an event in the near future?"

"Course not, Mr. Rothenstein. I was simply . . ."

My attention was next drawn to a screen showing the statues of Christ and St. Avaro, the ones I'd been gazing at in person that afternoon. Several skycars were circling them and all at once Christ's beard exploded, went fragmenting across the dusk.

A tiny newsman in the foreground was saying, ". . . work begins on the awesome task of converting these out-moded icons into functional images of our two enlightened dictators, the benevolent Janota Twins. The brilliant General Manuel Janota and the equally brilliant General João Janota, who today signed the . . ."

"Hey, you're one melloroony of a lay!"

Twilight Malone, hands on hips, was standing at the foot of the floating circular bed I was collapsed on. I blinked at her. "Well, thanks. You mean, we've been—"

"Thrice." She rubbed her hands together. "That's a very macvouty quiffer you got on you, hon." She came around the big bed toward me. "I think we got time for one more swiftie before I got to get into costume for my midnight cast. So if—"

"Wait now, Miss Malone." I found I was capable of sitting up. "Don't take this as a lack of fondness for you or a symptom of a cavalier attitude, but I . . . I don't seem to recollect anything that went on between us."

"Sure, that's because of the concussion." She nodded, long red hair brushing at her bare black shoulders.

"Concussion? I've got a—"

"Only a mild one. Doc was of the opinion you'd be a little nutsoreeny for a few hours and then snap out of it," she said. "You wasn't too dopey for some—"

"Listen, could you tell me how long I've been here?"

"Ever since you clunked your poor cabezareeny on that flapping Grub Hut window this afternoon, hon." Twilight sat beside me, touched at my chest with slender fingers. "See, after you risked life and limb to save me, I figured I owed it to you to make sure you pulled through. One of the neatoroony things about being rich and fabled is I get to be a samaritan any old time I want." Tilting, she kissed me on the forehead. "You can stay long as you like, except you got to lie low whiles I'm on the air. Don't come wandering into the set with your doofer hanging out or—"

"Thing is, Miss Malone, I'm on a sort of mission," I told her. "This, pleasant as it apparently was, is deflecting me from my real course."

She frowned. "What sort of mission?"

"A personal one."

"Having to do with Special Agent Elizabeth Clarenson?"

"How'd you know about—"

"Whiles you was delirious you mentioned her quite a lot. Is that young lady important to you?"

"I came here to find her," I answered. "And I'm going to."

Twilight shook her head. "Give up the whole idea, hon."

"Why?"

"You'll only get killed," she said.

CHAPTER 8

Piper was glaring at the breakfast menu that was crawling across the display screen in the dining nook of our suite at the Sheraton-Avaro. "Grub-Bacon Style, Grub-Grandma's Hotcakes Style, Grub-Pork Chops & Gravy Style . . . How does one feast on something other than this ubiquitous swill?" He glanced up as I hesitated on the threshold. "You look as though you were run over by a landvan and thereafter assaulted by a band of sex-starved amazons, my boy. Where've you been?"

"Well, that's pretty much what did happen." I crossed the sunlit room, slumped into a floating plexisling. "Actually, I had an accident involving cracking my skull against a Grub Hut window. After—"

"Grub again," he said with a scowl. "That resurrected garbage is going to do us all in, one way or the other. But continue, Justin."

"Listen, Piper, I met Twilight Malone," I told him, leaning forward in my chair. "She knows more about what's going on in Erequay than Towers or anyone. Her network sent her down here last month to cover the war between the Janota Twins' forces and the rebels, so she—"

"Did you spend the night with the lass?"

"And the afternoon, most of it," I admitted. "Don't remember any of the afternoon, but if it was anything like the night I must've surely had a—"

"During your spell of intimacy with the statuesque

newsmonger, my boy, did you mention what we're up to?"

"I was delirious for a time, Piper. Twilight says I babbled quite a lot."

He rose up out of his glaz rumphug chair, came over to stare down at me. "Did you mutter about our true reason for being here?"

"About Beth? Sure, it's on my mind all—"

"Forget the lassie. I'm alluding to plan to sell several tons of Grub to certain black market capitalists."

"Don't think I did. Although Twilight did ask me why I'd been wearing a Child Salvation Corps uniform."

"Been wearing?"

"She had to undress me for the doctor."

"Not standard procedure for a head injury, m'lad."

"They thought I might be hurt elsewhere. In fact, I do have a bump on my—"

"What you're trying to convey to me, Justin, is you may well have, in a fit of passion, blurted all my innermost secrets to this dusky bimbo."

"Passion had nothing to do with it, damn it." I stood up, mad, facing him. "Maybe when I was dazed I mentioned something about this latest crooked flimflam of yours, but it—"

"It's *our* crooked flimflam."

"There's something else I want to talk over sometime," I said to him, striving to control my voice. "I've been thinking stealing food that's supposed to go to starving orphans isn't exactly my kind of—"

"Food? Who the bloody hell said anything about food? We're diverting a few truckloads of Grub. These poor benighted waifs are better off not having the stuff pumped into them."

"When you're starving Grub can taste—"

"Is Twilight Malone a practicing minister on the side?

You've certainly turned holy since putting the proverbial boots to her."

"It's probably because I know Beth is alive," I told him. "I feel stealing this food from little kids isn't—"

"Beth? Are you intending to reform because of her, my boy?" He laughed at me, face close to mine. "The same wench who's at this very moment inserting a shock device into the—"

"We don't know for sure she's directly involved in any of that business."

"Oh, so? I was under the impression we did." Piper turned his broad back on me. "I'll have to forgo the rest of your sermon, and I'll pass on breakfast as well. I have an appointment shortly."

"Who with? Does Towers have more info—"

"Forget that girl for a bit," he said. "I have an audience with the Pope."

"Which Pope?"

"*The* Pope," he replied. "Pope Sun Ming I, the pontiff of the Roman Catholic Church, the ruler of Sacred Rome, the—"

"You're going to con the Pope as part of this food scam?"

"He figures in my plot, yes." Piper carefully smoothed his moustache. "As the first Oriental Pope in the long and glorious history of Mother Church, he's acutely aware of how the minorities of the world are suffering."

"I saw him on the news last night," I said. "Arriving in São Avaro in that gem-encrusted skyvan, wearing realsilk clothes and more finger rings than two bordello piano players."

"You seem to have grown more pious and more sacrilegious at the same time," Piper observed. "Be that as it may, I want you to wait here until I return. Then we have to go to the São Avaro orphanage, in our benevolent uniforms, to–"

"Haven't you heard what I've been telling you? I think Twilight can help us. She can help locate Beth. So I want–"

"She can help us right into a cozy homelike cell," Piper warned. "A woman with all the international connections that lady has must be tied in with one or more intelligence agencies. You tell her about what we're up to as regards Beth and the next time you wake up there'll be a Dozerizer attached to–"

"I trust her."

Piper shook his head. "At your age I might have myself."

"What you want me to do is sit on my duff until you need me in the food swindle. After that's all squared away you'll, maybe and perhaps, help me do what I'm really interested in. Hell, you're trying to con me, Piper."

His left eye narrowed. "I don't con my friends," he said evenly. "You're one of the few such I have."

"Come on, you don't really care what happens to me or–"

"We'll have to talk about this later, my boy. Right at the moment I needs must–"

"We'll talk about it never!" I pushed by him and went striding out of the suite.

CHAPTER 9

Nine men died out in the bright afternoon, or possibly it was ten. Angry, thinking about myself, I didn't pay much attention to the public execution. I only passed the edge of the ceremonies, actually, on my way to the bay.

They had them, stripped naked, up on a narrow plaz platform raised about ten feet above one of the city's colorful plazas. A sizzling force screen kept the captives herded together, prevented them from trying to leap to freedom. Federal skyvans were cruising over the thick crowd of spectators, belly-speakers talking about, ". . . *malfeitors* . . . *rebelião* . . . *justiça* . . ."

Captive rebel guerrillas, being killed as an example to would-be malcontents. The executioners used laser guns on the naked men, shooting down from the hovering skyvans. They sliced them into bloody chunks.

I hardly glanced at the slaughter, muttering about my own problems as I pushed through the edge of the crowd. I heard sudden screams and then the silence.

"Watch the elbows, crum."

I'd nudged into a vendor who was offering Grub-on-a-stick from the neowick basket slung over his hairy arm. Giving him an apologetic grin, I thrust three fingers, stiff, into a soft part of his lower gut.

"Arp," he said.

Juvenile thing to do, but I was angry and preoccupied.

The vendor stumbled out of my way. I strode on, leaving the packed plaza behind. The circling vans must have done something else, a stunt maybe, because the spectators began applauding.

The sand along the public stretch of bay was tinted a warm and unreal gold. I slowed, stopped, and tugged off my boots. I went walking barefooted across the sand. They had some other additives in it as well, because it was cold underfoot.

I moved across the cold sand, not much noticing the tan girls and wide-shouldered guys sprawled around. Well, one girl in a plyobrief with frontal vents did distract me briefly.

In less than half a minute I was back to rerunning my morning's conversation with Piper.

"Letting me down," I was saying inside my head. "Okay, he does have a scam to work . . . and I sort of did promise to help him. But, Christ, Beth is more important . . . he said he'd help me find her . . . Listen, he wouldn't even have promised that if he didn't suspect there was a way to turn a buck in all this . . . Sure, there's something behind all this, about why Beth isn't really dead . . . Piper'll come up with a scheme to make it pay off . . ."

Far out over the water some skysleds, mostly stark white and gleaming red, were skimming. Guys were dropping from them, diving down into the water with enormous and enthusiastic splashes.

All these years, and three years seemed a hell of a long time, I'd thought she was dead.

None of this made much sense.

I could remember talking to her father. A small man, faded and tired-looking, who ran a postal telop machine in the Loop Stockade. Standing in the Nabe hospital on the outskirts of the Chicago Citistate and hearing him tell me she had a rare viral cancer, fast-acting. No cure yet. It would kill her in weeks, or maybe less. I felt very cold, inside especially.

They let me see her and you could sense death. She was gaunt, the hollows under her eyes so damn deep and dark. The veins on her arms made crazy red and black tracks, her skin had a damp, yellowish touch.

Beth's smile was still there. When she used it on me, I started to cry. Hell, I knelt beside her floating white bed and I blubbered. I was seventeen, remember. What exactly I told her I'm not sure. Something about how much I loved her, had since we'd met nearly two years before at the Nabe 230 Rehab Center. About how this wasn't fair and maybe we could get a specialist. You know, all the dumb things you babble when there's absolutely nothing that can be done.

Inside I was cursing my father, Jake Brinkman, who'd left us dumped in the shadow of the Chicago Citistate years ago. He took off and my mother had to support us from then on with, I didn't admit then, not much help from me.

If he'd stuck, we might be doing a lot better now. There might be enough money to . . . I don't know, to buy Beth's life back somehow. To do some damn thing.

I saw her only once more. That was when she was dead and I stood by her coffin.

Her weary father, done up in a nearly new two-piece black sundaysuit, thrust his head over the rim of the coffin to kiss her cold sunken cheek.

I guess they expected me to do that too—kiss her goodbye. I couldn't.

I got out of the way, moved back to where Piper was standing near the wall of the Transition Service chapel. The coffin went rolling forward on its ramp, the automatic sad music started wailing out of the overhead speakers. A hole opened in the far wall and her coffin rolled through.

I saw the flames crackling inside there, saw them start to eat at her coffin. My back was turned before the wall shut on Beth.

There was nothing else to stay in the Chicago area for, so when Uncle Winsmith offered my mother a chance at a better job in Connecticut I voted to take it.

I really had loved Beth. I'd been certain she was gone forever.

Except she wasn't.

She wasn't even Beth Danner. She was Elizabeth Clarenson.

They'd conned me. Faked her death.

But why?

And, more important, who?

Nobody made a buck out of the deal. Her dad hadn't even had an insurance policy on her. Did they stage the whole business just for me, an unimportant Nabe kid?

"She's a government agent," I muttered. "She's not even Beth Danner. Well, you should have sensed that because you're not even . . ."

I felt very strange right then. My stomach gave a lurch. I felt extremely hollow.

Lowering myself to the cold golden sand, I struggled to grab back that idea I'd almost found. The one that made me suddenly feel I'd been bopped in the crotch by a 'bot cop.

No use, couldn't retrieve a thing.

The skysleds wheeled back and forth through the afternoon sky.

Twilight Malone, being annoyingly cryptic, had warned me to drop the search for Beth. I was damn certain Twilight knew a good deal more about what the Federal Overseers were up to in Ereguay and where Beth might be.

I stood up.

Twilight was going to tell me.

CHAPTER 10

Less than an hour after dawn we were careening through the outskirts of São Avaro, scattering clucking chickens, sleepy dogs, early risers, and a flock of shaggy animals I was pretty sure were goats.

"Dumbbell!" yelled Twilight Malone at a blindman who was executing a shaky backflip to keep clear of the path of her new silver landvan.

"*Marafona!*" he gasped as his narrow backside smacked into the dust.

"Hicks." Twilight had her red hair tied up in a plyoscarf, she was wearing tinted driving goggles. She sat at the wheel in a tense crouch, slim black fingers digging into the plaz padding, breasts perked up, nostrils slightly flared.

"I could take over the driving," I offered.

"Naw, studoroony, I love to drive. Helps me relax. Turdbowl!"

This last was directed at a black-shawled old grandmother who'd been trying to carry a head-held basket of oranges across the course of our roaring juggernaut.

The old woman dived, for a few seconds looking like the best juggling act the world had ever known, and then oranges, basket, and old lady smacked down on the weedy sidewalk. "*Marafona!*" she screamed at our retreating tail.

"Why all these sodkickers keep calling me that?"

From the back of our van came a snicker. "Eez because

you looks like zee hooker," said Manzano. "That eez what zee word she means."

Manzano was a plump guy of thirty some years, curly-haired, moustached. He had on a suit of green workalls with the SatNet-1 logo too large on the left breast pocket. According to Twilight, he was the local network trouble-shooter and had helped set up this morning's news mission.

Manzano was sharing the back of the jolting van with a robot camera. A mansize, manshape mechanism, olive-drab body and a vidcam for a head. "Could we perhaps have a little less joggling, Miss Twilight?" he requested out of the voice hole in his chest.

"Go degauze yourself, macfruity."

Manzano chuckled, tugging a map from his pocket. Actually it was a Grub Hut menu with a rough map penciled in the margin. "We eez gots *umo* hour more at least before we gets to where we eez going. Eez she okay eef I indulge een my hobby?"

"Go ahead, fatsoroony." Gritting her teeth, Twilight guided the newsvan clear of the last of the town and onto a wide dirt road which went cutting through a thick, tangled, and seemingly endless forest area.

Manzano, grunting, reached down to pick up his head-box TV. "Eez you a *sabão* fan, Senhor Breenkman?"

I glanced back as he fitted the box down over his round head. "Not sure."

"Aw, he's obsessed with soap operas," explained Twilight, hunching lower, eyes glaring at the dusty road ahead of us.

"I are only fanatical about two soaps," corrected Manzano, voice echoing inside his viewing box. "One is *A Otra Esposa de João* and *Amor e Sangre* is the *otra.*" Pudgy fingers tapped the top of the box near the cassette slot. "I has loaded seex episodes of *Amor e Sangre* een.

Book seexteen, Chapters Seven through Twelve. That was, as you may recall, senhor, the famous sequence wherein Dr. Marcus learns that young Rudy is actually a clone of his archrival, Knee Specialist Milman. Eet was also during theez fateful sequence that Seester Patricia of the Convent of the Tapdancing Madonna admitted she had been the surrogate mother of Chief Justice William Van Horn and that heez true father was not kindly old Professor Emerzon but a test tube now in the possession of the Senate SubCommittee on Executive—"

"Enough crapola," suggested Twilight, gunning the car up to a rattling hundred and twenty kiloms per.

"Pleez to begin." With another chuckle Manzano turned on his viewing unit.

"Whoops," said the camera, who'd been introduced to me as KC/55057. "Oughtn't we perhaps to slacken our speed, Miss Twilight?"

"Hooey."

I said, "He sounds as though he might be on the brink of going on the fritz, so slowing—"

"Are you a flapping expert on robotics?"

"I was, though only briefly."

"Maybe you ought to consider going back to that."

It had taken me several hours to persuade Twilight to let me come along on this assignment at all. I utilized every technique of persuasion I'd learned from Piper as well as most I'd picked up since working on my own in Connecticut.

When I arrived there after my angry rambling around the Ereguayan capital, she'd been very cagey. Suspecting she was trying to hide something, I pressed. Turned out Twilight had received, through the pudgy Manzano, a tip on the location of the guerrilla leader Beijar's captive sister. The network was anxious for her to get out there and investigate. Often Twilight's investigations involved her walking right into a tricky situation. If she pushed into this one I was fairly certain she'd find Beth someplace nearby.

"First," I said now as we bumped along, "I want to find Beth."

"That ain't so very flattering to me."

"Twilight, you know I admire and respect you," I assured her. "With Beth, though, it's different. I . . . you know, she's sort of my childhood sweetheart. I thought she was dead and gone and—"

"Daz very good," commented Manzano from the rear. "You ought to be on a soap, Senhor Breenkman."

"Concentrate on Dr. Marcus," I advised without looking at him.

Twilight swerved our vehicle to avoid what I took to be a tapir trying to cross the road. "Dumfug," she told him as we zipped by. "Ever occur to you, lovoreeny, that our U. S. Gov might not want anybody to know how come this sweetie of yours is back among the living?"

"Be that as it may, Twilight, I'm going to persist."

"Usual reason for faking a death would be to get her off one situation and over to a new assignment."

"Nope, that can't be it. Beth's my age, or a few months older," I said, watching the forest deepen into jungle. "She couldn't have been a government agent at that age."

Twilight laughed. "Wow, you very naïve for a tad who's such an expert in the sackoroony."

"You're telling me the Federal Overseers would use a seventeen-year-old girl like that?"

"They'd use a six-month-old baby or a fetus in a pickle jar if it served their purposes."

"Listen, I was with her an awful lot back then," I told her. "Saw her at the Nabe school, when I managed to attend, and almost every night. She couldn't have been working on any assignment then, Twilight. There wouldn't have been any time."

"Sure she could of."

"How?"

"If you was the assignment, hon."

CHAPTER 11

KC said, "Whoops."

The landvan shuddered once more, coughed, and died.

"Hell of a place to plant a tree." Twilight, unnecessarily, turned off the ignitswitch. "Okay, let's us unload."

I was rubbing at my elbow, the one that had whammed into the door during our sudden halt. "This is our destination?"

"Why else would I of parked here, macvooty?" She opened her door with a kick of her tan boots, hopped out into the tree-circled little clearing.

"Parking?" I eased out my side of the newsvan. "That was what this last maneuver was?"

"You getting as bad as this pansy camera, all the time heckling my driving." She started across the high yellow grass to the trees.

"We're here, Mr. Manzano," the robot camera announced politely.

"*Momento,*" the network troubleshooter said. "I wan' for to see zee part where Dr. Cox learns he was genetically engineered by–"

"Thought it was Dr. Marcus," I said.

"Oh, he died two chapters ago of radiation poisoning brought on by a nuclear accident which occurred during his sentimental visit to his old hometown of Cedarville Center in the heart of–"

"Hey, detach that dingus from your noggin and come on over here," urged Twilight.

"*Sim, sim,* I are coming." He was having some difficulty getting the box off. "I got for to lose weight or buy a new machine."

With assists from me and the robot, Manzano freed his head. His hair was askew, matted.

"Come on, Manzano, trot," called the impatient Twilight.

He hurried through the grass to her side. "What are zee trouble?"

"Look down there, schmucko." Angry, she was pointing through the palm trees.

"Ah, yes. They are mos' impressive."

"You told me the raid was for high noon. But this, clunkoroony, ain't no high noon. This ain't even high nine o'clock in the flapping morning."

Manzano was consulting the scribbles on his menu margin. "What you know about that? Theez don' says twel', she say eight." He rolled his eyes. "So they are late instead of early. How about that one?"

I was with them by now, gazing through the trees. Down the slanting hillside, about a quarter mile away, was a city block. One lone block with just seven office buildings built around a public square. Up on a pedestal in the center of the plaza stood a twice mansize statue of one of the Janota Twins. "This is Selva Grosso?" I asked. "The new capital of Ereguay."

"Oh, they runned out of money long time ago, cause of the rebellion," explained Manzano. "This are all they build, nobody she lives here no more."

In addition to the statue, I noted approximately thirty men in one-piece camouflage suits stalking across the square. They were armed with laserifles and stunrods.

"How come those camouflage suits are pink, purple, and orange?"

"The rebs raided a government quartermaster post," said Twilight. "Some clunkoroony fairly high in the Janota regime is color-blind and ordered fifteen gross of the things."

"So those are rebels down there?"

"They's too slim and well-groomed to be gov troops."

"What we're witnessing is a rebel raid on the place where Beijar's sister is being held."

Twilight nodded absently. "KC, can you film this from up here, hon?"

"Well, I'm certainly not going to go traipsing down there and get my tooshy shot off." The robot camera reached up to adjust one of his lenses. "No problem, Miss Twilight."

I took hold of her arm. "This is really what you came out here for, isn't it? You had a tip the guerrillas were going to raid this hideaway."

"Course I did, hon." She shoved her camera closer to the trees. "Remember I warned you not to tag along, but you was stubborn."

"I thought there'd be a chance to approach the place quietly," I said. "Then I'd be able to slip inside to see Beth."

"That wouldn't grab nobody's flapping attention on my newscast," she informed me. "What they got to have is action and noise."

The rebels opened fire on the building opposite General Janota's rear end. It was a three-story structure, overgrown with some kind of large-leaved creeping vines. A second after the lasers started biting into the front of the place a dozen or more big yellow birds went scattering up off its slanting glaztile roof.

"Jesus, they'll kill everybody in there."

"Nope, this is only to scare the FO agents and the army folks," Twilight assured me.

The firing kept on. Pieces, large chunks sometimes, were being sliced clean off the building.

There was some fire returned from inside, mostly from the second level. Not much, giving me the impression there weren't more than six or seven people inside there.

"They thought they was safe here," said Twilight.

"Nobody come here no more," added Manzano.

"Damn it, they'll kill Beth." I started forward.

"They ain't going to kill nobody." Twilight tried to pull me back, clutching my uni tunic.

I yanked free, ran. After I dodged between two rows of thick palms I was out in the open. My plans for what to do next weren't exactly crystal clear. All I knew was I had to get down there to where Beth was, to stop them from hurting her.

Maybe it was because I was still wearing my Child Salvation Corps uni and they mistook me for a Fed soldier. Maybe it was simply because I came galloping down the mossy hillside to dash right into the middle of their rescue operation.

Whatever the reason, two of the rebs turned their stunguns on me and fired before I could blurt out a single damn word.

For a few seconds I didn't notice any change, then I suddenly became acutely aware of my bones. I could feel my whole and entire skeleton, and I had the strong impression it was trying to dig its way out of my body. Every single bone I possessed began to ache and throb and sing.

My jaw commenced wagging. I chomped at the air over and over. I discovered I had ceased to breathe and I was absolutely certain my lungs were drying up and dusting away to nothing.

For some reason I decided I could fly. I was able to raise my arms and flap them once before diving straight into an enormous patch of black oblivion.

CHAPTER 12

I saw my father.

He was a long way off, in a large dome room. Beyond its tinted glaz walls stretched an autumn forest, rich with crimson, golden, and earth-toned leaves.

My father wasn't alone. I could see three other men in the big office with him. Their conservative two-piece biz-suits were gray. That much I could make out. But I couldn't focus on their faces at all, those remained blurred.

I was running along a see-through corridor that arched over the New England woodland. My father had disappeared when I was around three, now I had found him again. All these years I'd hated him for what he'd done. This was my chance, finally, to tell him what I felt.

I kept on running along that corridor, aware I could see through several other buildings. Big ones that were part of some kind of factory complex.

No matter how hard and fast I ran, I couldn't get any closer to him. I wanted to, needed to talk to him. Ask him why he'd left us, if it was because of me.

The three gray men were going to do something bad to him, going to hurt my father.

That's really why I was running, to stop them from hurting him.

Except I couldn't ever get any nearer. My lungs ached, my legs were needled with pain.

I wasn't going to reach him in time. They had kilguns drawn, were circling him.

He turned toward me. I saw his face.

It wasn't my father at all. Not the grim, weathered man in the faded tri-op picture in my mother's bureau. Not Jake Brinkman.

I had to help him anyway. Keep them from killing him.

I'd call out a warning. There wasn't time to reach his side.

"Look out! Dad, they're going to kill you!"

They were gone—my father, the gray men who meant to take his life away. The huge dome of an office, the surrounding woods. All gone.

I saw now a stretch of damp stone wall smeared with blackish mildew.

And I saw Beth.

"You really fouled this one up," she said.

When I tried to stand up, her image suddenly went hazy. Pain raced across my skull, my legs made creaking noises. "Beth," I managed to say, voice weak.

She crossed the cell, pulling me up without much tenderness and propping me against the nearest slimy wall.

There was dirty straw thick on the floor. Sprawled on it was a small white-haired man in a one-piece labsuit. When I noticed the guy I asked, "Is he dead?"

"That's Dr. Dozer. He's been stunned, same as you were."

She was just as I'd remembered her. Older now, her auburn hair a shade darker, her slanting cheekbones slightly more noticeable. She had on tan slax, a white sleeveless tunic that was streaked with green stains. She had a gunbelt, too, its holster open and gaping. "Beth, I don't unders—"

"Oh, you should have stuck in the Nabes," she said,

moving back from me. "You and that thick-witted con-man buddy of yours."

I took a few careful breaths. "Listen now," I told her, my voice sounding almost like my own. "I guess you don't owe me a warm and sentimental welcome. I don't know what the protocol is for people who've returned from the dead. But I'm not going to listen to any bitching lecture from you either." I paused, wanting very much to take hold of her but refraining. "I love you, you know, and I've been moping around for three damn years believing you were dead and done for. And, Christ, you aren't. Okay, I saw you alive and I made up my mind to find you again. I don't have to apologize for that."

She stood watching me. "You shouldn't have come hunting after me."

"Then maybe you shouldn't have come back to life."

She turned her slim back to me. "I didn't want to go anywhere near Connecticut," she said. "This was an emergency mission, though, so I had no choice. If you—"

"You knew where I was?"

"Yes, I've always kept track."

"Why?"

She didn't answer for several long seconds. "Part of the job."

"What job? What does FO have to do with me?" I crossed the dingy straw, almost tripped over the unconscious old scientist, and put a hand on her shoulder. It was the first time I'd touched her in three years.

She reached up, brushed my cheek with her fingertips. She moved into my arms, hugging at me, pressed her head against my chest. "Damn it to hell," she murmured.

I held on to her. "Doesn't matter what kind of act you were putting on. You loved me, I know it."

"Maybe so." She pushed back, eyes misted. "Doesn't make any difference at this point."

"Can't you explain to me what–"

"I did something stupid, Justin. Back then. I became fond of you," she said. "I was only twenty, but even so–"

"Twenty? You were seventeen."

"That's only what we made you believe." She touched her left breast. "I'm almost twenty-four now, older than you by near four years."

"Hell, that's not much of a gulf."

"I've thought sometimes since then that what we did to you . . . well, it wasn't very admirable, but I . . . They never told me the real reason. I'm fairly sure of that." She shook her head. "They lied to my father, too. Although he still won't admit it. He's too stubborn to acknowledge the possibility he was conned into processing you."

"Wait now," I said. "Your father worked for the postal corporation. What could he have had to do with . . . processing me?"

"You never met my actual father," she said. "Danner was just another Federal Overseers agent."

"Your real father is named Clarenson?"

"Roger Clarenson, yes. He's done quite a lot of work for the United States Government over the years. It was through him I got recruited into FO."

"His specialty is processing? What does that involve?"

One of her booted feet dug at the straw on the cell floor. "Our government quite often has people who have to be given new identities," she said, eyes avoiding mine. "Sometimes, too many times, they also wish those people to forget certain things, certain classified bits of information, and so on. You process them, give them new faces, a whole new identity. You work, which was one of my father's specialties, on their brains, make sure they do forget. You can also work it so they remember things that never happened. You build a new sort of person, with brand-new memories. Expensive, but our government has always thought it more acceptable to modify people than to murder them. Usually."

I had both hands to my face, was poking at it. "What are you telling me, Beth? That I was processed that way?"

"Yes, that's exactly what I am telling you."

"They fooled with my looks, with my mind?"

"Until four years ago," she said slowly, "there was no such person as Justin Brinkman."

CHAPTER 13

"Who am I then?"

Beth moved as far away from me as she could in the small cell. "It's really," she said, "not going to do you much good. The way you were processed, it's like erasing your other identity. There's no way, probably, you can return to—"

"Tell me anyway."

"You're Josh Kingsmill," she said finally. "At least that's who you were before you went through my father's lab."

"Kingsmill," I said, frowning. "I'm not part of *the* Kingsmill family?"

"You are, yes."

"Come on, Beth, you're trying to con me again. I couldn't be one of them," I insisted. "I grew up in the Nabes, never had enough money, scuffled since I was—"

"Justin, you grew up in New England," she told me. "Don't you understand, all those memories you have of your childhood in the Nabes are false? Even the way you think you met me, that's not a real memory."

"My father, Jake Brinkman. I know he left—"

"There never was a Jake Brinkman. My father made him up, or rather his BG computer did when it fashioned a new ID dossier for you."

"And Rose Brinkman?"

"FO and other agencies have people on file, people who're willing to cooperate in these identity switches,"

Beth explained. "Rose Brinkman was one, so was her brother Winsmith."

"You mean they knew all the time I wasn't—"

"No, they were processed, voluntarily, so they thought your past was as real as you did."

"Too bad you didn't fix Winsmith to be a little more cordial to me." I crossed the straw to where she was standing. "How much of it is real? Anything?"

"We placed you in that Chicago Nabe roughly three and a half years ago. Anything you remember from then on is what really took place."

"Why were you there, pretending to be my sweetheart and all?"

"Sometimes a new identity doesn't quite take. It's our policy to observe the subject until we're satisfied he's settled into his new life."

"That's all we had? You were doing your job, keeping tabs on me."

"I told you I'm fond of you," she said. "I didn't have to stay so close, nor so long."

"Why'd you die?"

She hesitated. "That was mostly my father's idea," she answered. "He felt I was becoming too involved with one of the subjects. When it was clear you'd be Justin Brinkman for the rest of your days, he ordered me off the assignment."

"Pretty drastic way to transfer you."

"The fake death was to keep you from trying to track me down. If I'd only moved away, you'd surely have . . . you might have done exactly what you did now. Followed me, come barging right into a new mission and screw it all up."

"They should have killed me, then I wouldn't have made trouble for anybody."

"Whoever ordered this done, Justin, didn't want you dead."

I took hold of both her shoulders. "Who was that? I don't understand why the Federal Overseers wanted—"

"This was arranged through FO, but as a favor to someone else."

"Who?"

She pressed her lips together, saying nothing.

I think I shook her. "Beth, who had this done to me?"

"We were told," she said, "the request came from your father."

Letting her go, I said, "My father? You're talking about my real father?"

"David Kingsmill."

"But why?"

"We were told you'd done something, something pretty awful. They wanted you to disappear and this seemed the best out for the family."

"Something bad. Something terrible enough to justify destroying my identity. What the hell was it?"

"I don't know. I never knew."

"You're an FO agent. You have access to—"

"There was no reason for my—"

"But you did look, you did try to find out."

"I was interested in you, even after I had to leave," she said. "I even tried to contact your father, but by then he was dead."

"Looks like I'm never going to get together with my real father, be he Brinkman or Kingsmill." I shook my head, then thought of something. I commenced laughing.

"What is it?"

"Just recollected where most of the vast Kingsmill fortune comes from," I said. "They own Grub."

"That's one of the Kingsmill subsidiaries."

"Piper's been striving to divert a few truckloads of the

stuff," I said, grinning. "Here I am heir to the whole damn Grub empire. I can *give* him a couple tons of it."

Beth warned, "You'll never be able to prove any of what I've told you. I've seen enough of these ID switches to be certain of that."

"Is that why you keep calling me Justin and not Josh?"

"You don't seem like a Josh to me."

I thought about the matter. "Nope, and I don't feel like one either. I'll stay Justin for now."

"I can't tell you what to do, but I really don't think you ought to approach the Kingsmills at all," she said, concern showing on her face. "See, I don't think we were ever given the real reasons for what was done to you."

"What do you suspect?"

"There was, still is, something going on," she said. "I'm darn near certain the Kingsmill clan is fooling with something large and dangerous."

"Such as?"

"I don't know."

I kicked at the stone wall. "Meanwhile I seem to be entangled in your current assignment," I said. "Did you really come down here to torture some girl who—"

"Dr. Dozer's techniques are a long way from torture," she said. "If you knew what kind of man Beijar was, what his rebels have done to—"

"Red, white, and blue propaganda."

"Oh, have you learned the truth about Ereguayan politics from shacking up with Twilight Malone?"

"You know about that too."

"Some," she admitted. "Although we obviously didn't suspect that idiotic newsperson was going to bust into our interrogation setup."

"You didn't know about the guerrillas either."

"No, the security people in the Janota regime are dimwits. We shouldn't have relied so much on them."

"Was Twilight captured along with us?"

"No, she got away far as I know, she and the whole load of your media cronies."

"How about your sidekick, Oxner?"

"He's dead."

I wasn't sorry. Even though I'd never met the damn guy, I'd been considering him a rival. "The rebs did that?"

"Of course. They've kept the doctor and me around, I imagine, to use in future negotiations," she said. "As for you, Justin, I'm not sure why they didn't kill you."

"Well, if they believe I'm really a Child Salvation Corps officer, they may figure to swap me for a few more tons of Grub."

"You should have stuck in Connecticut."

"Sure, that would have been less embarrassing for you and your pop and the FO, not to mention the whole and entire damn Kingsmill family. But I . . . hey!" I'd remembered something and my face took on a slightly goofy aspect.

"Now what?"

"While I was unconscious I had a dream," I told her. "Except possibly it wasn't, it might have been a memory. Something from my real life."

"About what?"

"This had to do with my father getting killed. Could I have witnessed that, during my Josh Kingsmill phase?"

"Unlikely, since he didn't die until long after you were processed."

"Is that something you're dead sure about?"

"It's possible, I suppose, they could have lied about when he actually died. Your father wasn't the most visible of the three ruling Kingsmill brothers." Beth ran her forefinger over my chin. "There could be a reason, a damn good one, for getting rid of you. Or at least of your memories."

"Something I'll have to look into when we get out of here."

"Justin, I'm trying to tell you not to—"

"Listen, I found you," I said. "Now I've got to find myself."

CHAPTER 14

I joined Dr. Dozer on the straw.

Hadn't intended that, but the rebel in the camouflage suit proved a lot tougher than I'd anticipated. You don't expect a guy in a pink, purple, and orange ensemble to be all that formidable.

My plan, improvised when the thickset guard brought in our evening meal, was to jump him. I'd swipe his stungun and keys, hustle Beth and myself out of there.

The plan didn't work.

He tossed me over his shoulder and smack into the stone wall without even upsetting the food tray he was carrying.

I hit the mildewed stones with an impressive thunk, slid down to tumble over into a dizzy heap next to the still-groggy scientist.

"Your dinner tonight she are Grub *com carne,*" announced the big guard as he set the tray on the straw. "Is very tasty, an' good for you. *Boa noite.*"

"Ninny," observed Beth as soon as he was gone. "Why'd you try that?"

I gathered my wits, pushed myself to a kneeling position. "It was intended to be the start of a brilliant escape."

Sitting on the straw cross-legged, she picked up one of the glaz bowls of food and a plaz spoon. "Do you know where we are?"

"In a cell."

"But where's the cell?"

I gave an uninformed shrug. "That particular detail of our imprisonment I don't know."

"One thing you have to learn, Justin, is not to make a move until you know exactly where you are and what to expect," she told me. "Suppose you had overpowered this lout. We dash into the corridor and then what?" She tried a spoonful of the spicy Grub, wrinkled her pretty nose.

"I'd use his stungun on any opposition."

She hesitated over a second spoonful. "My notion is they flew us quite a distance from the Selva Grosso hideaway," she said. "There are some ruins deep in the jungle, the remains of Indian temples and such. We've suspected that Beijar's using them as a base."

"We're there?"

"Seems a good possibility," she replied, finally swallowing the second spoonful of Grub *com carne*. "Meaning if we did manage to get out of here, we'd be faced with a nice long trek through the jungle."

"We could swipe a skycar."

"Maybe."

I stood, crossed the cell to situate myself on the straw beside her. "Suggest an alternate."

"They're probably going to use the doctor and me as hostages, to swap with the Janota brothers for some of their own people who're in the São Avaro lockups." She returned her bowl to the tray. "Somewhere along the way we ought to have a fair chance to make a break. What we better do now is wait, see what's going to transpire."

"You're asking for more patience than I've got," I said. "Besides, they sure aren't going to use me in any trades. I could end up defunct."

"They'd have knocked you off by now if that was their plan."

"Sitting around in this ruin, or whatever it is, is not my idea of—"

"Aha! We'll simply cut through the stone walls."

Beth and I both turned to stare at Dr. Dozer. The rumpled old scientist was conscious, on his hands and knees.

"Beg pardon?" I said.

He shook his head several times, treating it as though he expected something to rattle inside. "I always carry a minilaser concealed in my boot."

"Boots are handy places to carry stuff," I agreed. "Your trouble, however, is—"

"Oops, my boots no longer appear to be on my feet." He wiggled his stubby toes, scattering straw.

"They searched us all while we were out," I told him. "Your boots were apparently so loaded with concealed gadgets, they kept them."

Dr. Dozer settled into a sitting position. "Well, then, we must blast our way to freedom." He reached into his labsuit. "I always carry a pellet of miniblast in my armpit. In less than a jiffy we'll . . ."

You could tell from his sagging expression the explosives were gone. "Beth suggests we just wait," I said.

"I don't believe we've met, young man," said Dozer. "I am Dr. Leo Dozer, Chairman of the Department of Practical Science at the L. Ron Hubbard Memorial Campus of Yale II."

He held out a knobby little hand. I shook it. "I'm Justin Brinkman, more or less."

Dozer said, "We'll be forced to eat the door."

"Nibble our way out?"

He was tugging at his scrambled white hair. A large patch came free from his dome of a skull. "I always carry a herd of mutant minitermites in a specially designed . . . Oh, nertz!"

"The rebels were pretty thorough, doctor," Beth said sympathetically.

"There is still my knee!" Hopping to his feet, he began rolling up his trouser leg. "This knee, young man, is quite plausible, don't you think?"

It was a knobby, pocked thing with a very believable little scab on it. "The thing's fake?" I inquired. "We worked in Chicago once with a very gifted pickpocket who had a fake elbow he used to—"

"My knee is cleverly fashioned from synskin and aluminum," Dr. Dozer said as he unscrewed it. "The basic principles of its brilliant design I've never dared patent for fear of letting my rivals have even a hint of how it was done. I can assure you there are several large prosthetic houses in the world who'd dearly love . . . Oh, futz!"

The small compartment concealed behind the false knee was quite obviously empty.

"I was counting on the elecdrill I carry there. This is very vexing." Dr. Dozer slammed his knee shut. "Here I slave and strive, toil untold hours to perfect these gadgets. The sole object of all that labor is to provide myself with the means of escaping the most unexpected and perplexing of challenges to my safety and security. Very disheartening to have those untutored guerrillas do such a . . . Aha, but wait!" He went shuffling into a corner. "If you'll turn your back, Agent Clarenson, I'll produce the teenie-weenie laserod I had the foresight to insert in my anus."

Masking her eyes with her fingers, Beth said, "Bet they found that one too."

Anxiously I watched the old scientist wiggle out of his labsuit, drop it around his knees, real and unreal. Lowering his all-season boxer shorts, he proceeded to probe. "Any luck?" I asked.

"I think I've . . . No, darn it! Even the laserod has been confiscated."

Dr. Dozer writhed back into his clothes, bent to wipe his fingers on a wad of damp straw. "I'll have to invent something on the spot," he decided. "Let's see, we have straw, rock, slime . . ."

"Maybe you ought to eat something," Beth said to me, nodding at the three bowls of Grub.

An oily scum had formed on the surface of the chili as it cooled. "Not hungry."

"If you're going to keep tackling our guards, you ought to build up your—"

"Listen, Beth, I may not be as efficient as an FO agent, I completely forgot to stuff a spare laserod up my butt, still, I don't need you to—"

"Sorry, didn't mean to be bitchy. I keep forgetting how young you are. In a few—"

"I'm not young," I said loudly. "I'm old beyond my years, street-wise and jaded."

Beth smiled, stretched out a hand and touched mine. "It's not bad to admit you don't have the experience an older—"

"Quit patronizing me." I jerked my hand away, stood up.

A knock sounded on the cell door. Then a guard asked, through the thick wood, "Hey, you wan' some spiritual guidance?"

Beth scowled. "You can take your—"

"Wait," I cautioned, a hunch taking hold of me. I eased close to the door. "What sort of guidance?"

"I gots a bishop out here offering to bless all you prisoners."

"Which bishop?"

Another voice replied, "Why, my boy, the Bishop of São Avaro, no less."

"Yeah, I'd love him to say a few well-chosen prayers for me. Come on in, please, your holiness," I invited.

Locks rattled and groaned, the wooden door creaked outward.

Piper, done up in some very impressive purple and gold robes, came, smiling beatifically, into our cell.

CHAPTER 15

"How come you're a bishop?"

"Originally I was going to try to convince them I was the Pope, except I've never done a very convincing Chinaman."

"Ten *minutos,* your grace," the rebel guard told Piper before closing him in our cell with us.

"Thank you, my son."

"Why'd you quit being the Child Salvation Corps officer?"

"Never does to stick to one guise too long," answered Piper. "Besides, my boy, this Holy Joe getup works wonders when you're trying to sneak two vanloads of borrowed Grub through the firing lines."

"Hello, Piper," said Beth, none too warmly.

"Ah, the phoenix of the FO." He gave her a fair sampling of several of his best grins and smiles. "You're even lovelier in your current reincarnation, my dear."

"You look about the same," she said, "although a lot thicker around the middle."

"Part of my disguise," he said, patting his stomach. "Enough of these tearful reunions, however, and on to the real purpose of my dropping in. I'm here to get you poor unfortunates out of this joint."

"How'd you know we–"

"Some of these guerrilla chaps, while ideologically

sound, are a trifle boastful," he said. "Whilst I was collecting for the Grub I'd delivered, they couldn't refrain from mentioning the lovely lady secret agent and the callow CSC youth they'd recently acquired, along with a noted old academic. That must be you, sir."

"Dr. Leo Dozer." In the corner the doctor bowed slightly. "And you are?"

"This is Piper," I told him. "Listen, Piper, I've found out quite a bit about myself."

"From our distaff Lazarus here?"

"Mostly, and I've been remembering a few things on my own."

"Justin, it's maybe not very wise to share what you know with a man like—"

"Nonsense, Elizabeth. I'm the closest friend he's got and, I might add, the only one who's stood by him through thick—"

"Stuck by him and used him," Beth accused. "Dragged him into one shady scheme after another, turned him into a—"

"Hold off," I told the two of them. "They're only going to give Piper a few minutes with us. Let me, as quick as I'm able, fill him in and then we'll talk about escaping."

Adjusting his robes around him, Piper said, "Proceed."

Very rapidly, talking fast as I could, I gave him a gloss of what I'd learned since stomping out of the hotel in São Avaro.

When I'd concluded, Piper steepled his fingers under his chin. "The heir to the Kingsmill fortunes?"

"So we think."

Piper put a ringed hand on Beth's shoulder. "You're not scamming, lass?"

She shrugged free of his touch. "No, although you'd better not try to—"

"All I intend to do is see this lad receives what's legitimately due him."

"With a nice hunk of it for yourself," Beth said. "Don't you understand that if you go anywhere near the Kingsmills they'll only hurt him? For some reason, they want him lost to the world. If the processing doesn't do it, they may well try something more certain."

"I have no intention of bearding these tycoons," said Piper. "Not yet."

I nodded at the door of our cell. "How about getting us out?"

"There's a possibility I can spring you, Justin," he answered. "As well as the young lady here. All three of you will present a real problem, one to challenge to the fullest—"

"You can forget about me and Dr. Dozer," Beth said. "Concentrate on Justin."

I stared at her, puzzled. "What the hell are you—"

"I'm on an assignment," she reminded. "Part of that involves looking after the doctor."

"Okay, so we'll figure a way to get all three of us out."

"Nothing's going to happen to me," she said. "The guerrillas won't kill me or Dr. Dozer. Staying with them I may be able to learn some—"

"But I just found you." I caught her hand. "Now you're telling me—"

"I'll find you again," she said. "I promise. I'm not certain what they have in mind for you, so if Piper can actually get you clear of them—"

"No, nope, not at all. I'm going to stick with you."

"My boy, the young lass is making perfect sense. You have—"

"Time she is up, your sacredness." A new guard, with a laserifle slung over his shoulder, had opened the cell door. "That are enough blessing for now."

Giving him a Holier Than Thou #3, Piper made a few mystical signs in the air. "May the lord be with you, my children," he said. Lowering his voice, he added, "Stand by for a quick flit, Justin."

CHAPTER 16

The morning guard didn't give me any choice. "They's waiting," he said and jerked me up off the straw by my uni collar.

"Who's waiting?" I asked as I came fully awake.

Saying nothing further, he hurried me out into the corridor.

"What about the others?"

A second guard shut and locked the cell door on Beth and the old doctor.

"What time is it anyhow?" I inquired as the large guy quick-stepped me along a wide, shadowy stone hallway.

"Almos' time for zee seex o'clock mass."

"Mass? Listen, if that's what you roused me for, you made a big mistake. I'm a confirmed heathen who—"

"No use trying to fool us," my guard told me. "The Beeshop explained who you really is."

Piper. What the hell had he told the guerrillas to make them want to rush me to church services at the break of day?

Gray light showed at the end of the upslanting corridor. I could make out some of the designs on the stone walls, intricate and deep-cut carvings with coiling snakes and blazing suns intermingled.

"What was She like?" asked the guard.

We stepped out onto a flat stone plateau in the open morning air. There was nothing on its broad expanse except a very old stone altar of the sacrificial type and

Piper. Still clad in his bishop outfit, he was leaning with cupped hands to light the last of the squat votive candles which decorated the altar top.

"Who?"

"The Virgin. Did she glow?"

Piper was apparently attempting a variation of the Divine Miracle dodge. We'd done fairly well with that in the Evanston Redoubt once, though I couldn't comprehend how he was going to put it to use with the hundred or more guerrilla soldiers who were kneeling around on the stone steps leading up to this outdoor sacrifice spot.

"Oh, quite a bit," I replied. "Of course it was high noon when I had this miraculous visitation, thus the glare of the midday sun detracted from some of the luminescent effect."

"I understan'. An' did She truly float in the air?"

"Sure, a divine manifestation always floats," I said while we approached Piper. "There She was, Mary Herself, about ten feet up and—"

"The Beeshop, he says five feet."

"Well, it was a windy day. She got wafted around some, went from, say, something like three feet above the ground to a record high of fifteen," I improvised. "I tell you, my son, it was some miracle. My whole life has been changed for the better . . ." I moved away from the guard to stand close to the berobed Piper. "What the hell are you working?"

"*Dominus vobiscum,*" he intoned, making pontifical gestures with his ring-heavy fingers. "There lads required a mass to bring good fortune to their cause. I, as a high-ranking churchman, have been called upon to celebrate same."

"Can you fake a mass?"

"My boy, I can fake anything." He unexpectedly

kneeled, touching his forehead to the ancient stones. "*Per omnia et cetera.*"

I knelt, whispering my question. "Where do I fit in?"

"I told them I needed an altar boy, an able assistant." He rose again, hands lifting above his mitered head. "*Mea culpa.*"

"Why me?"

"Exactly what the leader of this belligerent bunch, yonder burly chap with full beard, laserbazooka, and plaz rosary beads, was most anxious to know," said Piper. "He offered me the services of several strapping young revolutionists, each versed in the lore of Sacred Rome and the sacrifice of the mass. I rejected the lot, explaining that rotting away in their very own foul dungeon was a CSC officer noted across the length and breadth of South America for his piety, religiosity, and all-around spotless outlook. On top of which, the lad had actually seen the famous Virgin of Tijuana. They were impressed, impressed enough to remove you from your cell."

"Damn it, Piper, I didn't want to leave there. Not unless Beth can come along. I've been trying to find her for—"

"Mass! Mass!" some of the kneeling guerrillas commenced chanting. "We want a mass!"

"Can't delay any longer." Piper picked up a cruet of red wine.

"Those are blood stains on the altar, aren't they?"

"Very antique blood."

"So far," I said. "What good, by the way, does it do me to assist you? Once this charade is over, they'll dump me back—"

"Last night, Justin . . ." He genuflected, raised the flask of wine on high. "Better hasten over onto my right. Kneel when I kneel, babble when I babble."

"Last night what?" I eased into place, kneeling, rising.

"I explored, after the rebels were safely locked in the arms of sleep and the guards were dozing. I explored these fascinating old ruins." He poured some wine into a golden goblet. "Matthew, Mark, Luke, John. You may recall I'm quite up on the subject of archeology."

"Yeah, I know you sold the lost treasure of King Tut at least four times."

"Seven times. Thus I was able to push through to the innermost recesses of these venerable ruins." He took a sip of wine. "Ugh! 2027, Brazilian port. A bad wine, a dreadful year. Praise be to god. At any rate, I quite soon found a nugget of information the resident guerrillas overlooked."

"What?" We both knelt and rose, muttering pious-sounding phrases.

"The priests of this temple, during its fun-loving human sacrifice days, had a method of arriving at this altar in such a way as to awe and impress the local devout."

"A secret passage?"

"Exactly, my boy. Located directly 'neath this altar."

"Holy moley." We both genuflected again.

"No doubt the stunt was accompanied by an impressive amount of smoke, to obscure the mechanics of it."

"Do we have smoke?"

Piper reached into his robes, produced a packet of green powder and palmed it. "I'm never without the ingredients for a bit of mysticifaction," he said. "When I holler, 'Ditch!', you come exactly where I tug you. Understand?"

"Sure, but what about Beth and—"

He gestured toward the candles. We were all at once engulfed in billows of acrid green smoke.

Some of the guerrillas got angry, began yelling, "What

gives?" An equal number, from the sound of them, were favorably impressed. "Eez a miracle!"

"Ditch!"

I couldn't see a damn thing. Piper grabbed me, pulled me downward. I felt myself stumbling down a stone stairway. Chill air closed in around me, along with a thick, musty darkness. I heard a heavy stone smack down above my head.

"Fortunately we're both in tiptop physical shape, unless your recent dallying with the media has sapped—"

"Where are we?"

"Underground, my boy, in a long-forgotten tunnel," Piper informed me. "I was about to suggest we run as fast as our little legs can carry us. In case, though the possibility is fairly remote, of angry pursuit."

"I'm not running anywhere until you explain how we take Beth."

"We don't. The young lady already explained to you she felt it her duty to remain with the famed ballbuster, Dr. Dozer, and see this adventure to its end."

"I don't care what she—"

"This passway runs express to a secluded patch of jungle a good two miles beyond the temple ruins," said Piper. "There's no way we can leave it to make a side trip to the cell."

"Then I'll have—"

"Beth promised you'd be able to find her again," Piper said, a trace of impatience in his voice. "If things go according to plan, you'll soon be acknowledged as a rightful member of the Kingsmill combine. Then you'll merely pick up the pixphone, give a ring to Wildman Woolinsky, the esteemed prexy of the U.S.A. After some polite badinage about the state of the union and conditions in the used car business, you bring up the topic of Beth. You tell

Woolinsky you'd appreciate his sending one of his lovelier FO agents out to your villa in–"

"No, Piper, I won't desert her for– Ooof!"

Right out of the blackness a fist came hurtling. It smacked into my chin. Hit me hard three more times. I started to fall and, as I was tumbling down, an unseen chop across the back of my neck put me out entirely.

CHAPTER 17

". . . one look tells all, Monsieur Éclair. His suit is a full ninety years old. Test the material, not too zealously, and you have tactile proof of the extreme authenticity of this exhibit. This suit was made in the United States in a long-ago time known as the World War Two period."

"Why such droll shoulders?"

"The fashion of the time. He is wearing what was known as a zoot suit."

"Ah, I have heard of such."

"Who has not? Once you exhibit the Cryptobiotic Man in Guy Éclair's Eclectic Circus, you'll be the sensation of Paris, monsieur, and of all France eventually."

"Might I poke him?"

"Do anything you like within reason. He'll soon be yours."

Somebody thrust a finger into my middle.

"He's been asleep since when?"

"The last century. 1943. Ninety years."

"He's been asleep as many years as the suit is old?"

"He put it on, was almost immediately struck by lightning in a picturesque American hamlet known as Spanish Harlem, and dropped at once into a deep coma. His adoring, hardworking parents kept him at home, in a very handsome though inexpensive real glass case until they were well into their seventies. Then, growing old as well as a bit tired of the novelty of an eternally sleeping son, they sold him to Colonel Bascom's Flea Museum."

"Fleas?"

"These were mutant fleas, M. Éclair, large as a—"

"It will not hurt if I spray him, just in case?"

"Not at all, sir."

"You know, Dr. Piper, I'm wondering if perhaps he doesn't appear too healthy, now I see him up close like this."

"Amazingly well preserved, that was how I described this splendid specimen when I displayed him to you via the pixphone."

"Might I pinch his cheek?"

"Do with the Cryptobiotic Man what you will."

Somebody pinched my cheek.

"Amazing state of plasticity, isn't there, M. Éclair? I, in all honesty, must tell you I haven't seen a body in such a beautiful state since Major Braff-Jarvis and I unearthed the mummy of the late King Tut's identical twin brother, but that's another story."

Somebody tugged at my ear lobe.

"Another thing which occurs to me, Dr. Piper, now the fires of enthusiasm lit in my bosom by your long-distance rhetoric have burned low, is that my patrons will find him dull. He merely sleeps."

"He doesn't sing and dance, no. He sleeps, an eternal and endless sleep. The São Avaro Curiosity Museum, whereat I was fortunate enough to purchase this amazing creature, informed me, and I have no reason to doubt their word, that the Cryptobiotic Man was their prime attraction."

"One wonders why they sold him then."

"Ereguay is in a very unsettled state, monsieur. Museums specializing in oddities are thought frivolous and are shunned by the ruling class. Whereas in Paris an attraction such as this one will draw in the traditional fun-loving Parisian—"

"You honestly believe people will flock to see this poor fellow sleeping away?"

"You must have thought similarly, M. Éclair, or you wouldn't have advanced us transportation money."

"In the past, Dr. Piper, you've provided me with some sensational acts. Elana the Bird Girl, for instance, did exceptionally well until she unexpectedly began to molt. Still—"

"What say we sign the final papers? Then you can lock up this impressive new attraction for the night."

"And he does nothing but sleep?"

"On and on."

I yawned, opened my eyes and sat up.

"*Mon Dieu!* What is this?" demanded M. Éclair, a small swarthy man with deep-cut rings beneath his bulging eyes and a lucite derby cocked on his hairless head.

"A rare scientific event!" exclaimed Piper, who was wearing a two-piece white suit of an obviously medical cut. "It's only too bad this didn't occur during tomorrow's show, M. Éclair. The publicity garnered would have been formidable. Cryptobiotic Man Awakens After Nearly a Century! Another Coup for Éclair!" He moved closer to the glaz table I was atop. "You wouldn't care, young man, to go back to sleep for a few more years?"

"He's of absolutely no use to me at all now," said the circus owner. "I advanced you five thousand trudollars for him asleep. Awake he's worth not a sou."

Patting my shoulder, Piper soothingly said, "This is the year 2033, my boy. That's going to take some getting used to, I know. You've had, you see, quite a long nap. This world you've awakened into is a far cry from the simple one you knew. I'd be more than happy to act as your guide and mentor until—"

"What'd you shoot into me?"

"A harmless tranquilizer, one more often used in preparing elephants for surgery," he explained out of the side of his mouth.

"We're in Paris?"

"I'll explain all later."

"I feel I must," put forth the circus owner, "have my deposit back, Dr. Piper. A wide-awake boy, even though he's ninety years old or more, is of no interest to the discriminating patrons of my circus and freak pavilion."

"Why, M. Éclair, this authentic zoot suit alone is worth the small amount you advanced."

"But this youth is wearing it, not me."

Piper helped me to stand up off the table. My legs felt very undependable.

"Very well, my policy is never to argue over a money transaction," he said. "Can you stand unaided, my boy? If you'll but wait until I settle accounts with our agitated friend here, I'll thereafter escort you outside to introduce you to the amazing Twenty-first Century." From an inner pocket of his white suit he produced a Banxbox. "Let's see now, that would be five thousand less carting, special handling, fumigation—"

"Am I sensing you don't intend to pay me back the total and entire amount, doctor?"

Piper gave him a wave of the hand and his Martyr's Smile #6. "Very well, you're absolutely right of course, sir." He punched at the tiny buttons on the Banxbox surface. "It was the renowned Dr. Piper solely who had the ill fortune to purchase one of the wonders of the world only scant hours before he decided to end a snooze of nearly a century's duration. No reason why you should be out of pocket, eh?"

"Exactly, my dear doctor."

A Chexform whirred out of the proper slot in the box. Grinning, Piper tore it off to pass to the circus owner. He took me by the elbow. "Young man, you've a great deal to catch up on. We'll begin with a stroll down the Boulevard Périphérique."

"I'd appreciate that, kind sir," I said in a humble voice. "You can tell me how the world has gone since I fell into my unfortunate trance."

"Exactly." He guided me toward the door of the office. "Good afternoon, M. Éclair."

Folding the Chexform away under his tunic, Éclair nodded us across the threshold. "If he should fall into another stupor," he called, "don't hesitate to bring him back. He might make an interesting attraction at that."

When we were down on the gray late-afternoon street, I said to Piper, "Okay, explain."

CHAPTER 18

"There below us is the Arc de Triomphe, my boy, always a must-see for the first-time tourist. Ah, and there we notice the well-known Eiffel Tower, or what's left of it after the 2019 troubles. In a moment, if you look sharp, you'll be able to catch a glimpse of Notre Dame Cath—"

"Why'd you drug me?" I was sitting, arms folded across the front of my zoot suit, in the passenger bucket of his skycar. I was ignoring the twilight Paris we were drifting over at an altitude of one thousand and six feet.

"To get you quickly out of Ereguay," he said. "It was imperative to get you to Paris as swiftly as possible. I knew if you were conscious you'd kick and scream. Therefore, after I decked you in the tunnel, I administered a shot of some stupefying fluid I happened to have on my person. And, voilà, you awake a day later in France."

"Suppose I hadn't awakened. Were you planning to leave me on display at that Éclair's circus side show?"

"Matter of fact, Justin, you revived somewhat ahead of schedule. I was calculating you'd sleep until after I took in my final payment from our derbied circus mogul." Piper punched out a landing pattern on the skycar dash. "I had you set, so I thought, to rise up around about midnight this evening. A few moments prior to that I'd have slipped deftly into M. Éclair's establishment and quickly spirited you away. As it is, I'm out the five thousan—"

"Come on, Piper. I was with you when you bought that fake Banxbox off a mec counterfeiter in Chicago."

"Well, yes, I did come out a few bucks ahead," he admitted as the car swooped down through the waning day. "You see, my boy, there I was in Ereguay with a sleeping lad on my hands and an urgent need to travel to Europe. Reluctant to spring for the fare necessary to get us across the water, I decided, after outlining several equally brilliant plans in my mind, to give M. Éclair the chance to pay the freight."

"Where'd you get this nitwit suit you stuck on me?"

"Authentic-looking, isn't it? Borrowed from an aging chorus boy in Stacy Towers' circle."

"Okay, fine, you got yourself a free ride to Paris," I said. "Now suppose you utilize your celebrated wits to get me the hell back to Ereguay. You forced me to abandon Beth at—"

"The young lady in question is no longer at the ruins."

"What'd they do to—"

"Whilst you slumbered, lad, an exchange was arranged, exactly as dear Lizzie anticipated," Piper told me. "She's now safely back in São Avaro."

"Even so, I have to see her. There's not a damn thing for me in Paris."

"On the contrary, you're going to find out the truth here."

The skycar, with a few very gentle bounces, settled to rest on a plazfalt landing area off the Rue de Rivoli.

"I know enough of the truth. I'm more interested in getting back to Beth so—"

"You only know what she told you."

"She wasn't lying, Piper."

"Nor, on the other hand, was she telling you all she knows."

"You've got no evidence she—"

"There are some people here in Paris it's important you

talk to. They're a very gifted bunch called the Gypsies. With an assist from them we can—"

"What? Fortune-tellers?"

"Not exactly." After unbuckling his safety gear, he flipped the door-open toggle. "If you really are Josh Kingsmill, then you control a large portion of one of the largest congloms in the world. Your late father held fifty-one percent of all Kingsmill stock. It passed on to your two uncles at his death, but only because you were listed as officially deceased as a result of a fatal skycar crash in the New Hampshire Zone," he said. "However, since you are very much alive, you can claim what is rightly yours. The Kingsmill empire is worth, at conservative estimate, seventy billion dollars."

"You've been busy nosing into things while you had me doped up."

"I asked a few useful and discreet questions here and there," he acknowledged, opening his door wide but not moving from the skycar. "You'll be in one nifty position to woo a government lady agent when you assume your true identity. With the complete control of billions of bucks, you can find out everything you've always wanted to know about Bess, as well as her slypuss of a father."

I looked away from him, out at the dusk. "Listen, the Kingsmills faked my death, wiped out my memory, and stuck a new ID on me," I said slowly. "Even though I don't know why they did that, I'm sure they're not going to take me back into the bosom of the family."

"Not at the moment, no," said Piper. "They'll have to accept and acknowledge you once you know enough. When you're certain why they did what they did to you, then you can move on the bastards."

"How're we going to find that stuff out, especially here in Paris?"

Piper dropped to the ground, stood grinning in at me.

"We simply ask the one person who knows everything that happened."

"Who's that?"

"You, my boy."

CHAPTER 19

"Are ya man enough to tackle me, buster?" inquired the huge figure blocking the doorway of the saloon.

"I could probably handle two of you," I told him, "except right now we—"

"Aw, a pansy! A milksop, lily-livered, whey-faced whelp of a wall-eyed mooncalf, is what you are, Percy." He shook a big sooty fist under my nose. "Me name's Socko an' I say I can beat ya to—"

"Move aside," Piper said to the big unkempt android. "We didn't come to P. J. Mechanix' Pub to use the amusement machines, Socko."

Socko shuffled his huge feet on the neosawdust, twisted his cap in his hands, and said, "Aw, I ain't gonna make me quota terday this way, Pipe."

Piper stuck three hundred-franc coins into the slot in the hulking android's broad chest. "This'll help."

"Don't ya wanna toss even a few punches?"

"Perhaps after our business is concluded, Socko, we'll return and mop up the joint with you."

"That'll be hunky-dory, Pipe." Grunting, the big coin-in-the-slot andy lumbered out of our way.

We entered P. J. Mechanix', a long narrow place down in the murky style of a last-century pub. Dark neowood walls, milky mirrors, low, beamed ceilings, murky air, packed with burly young guys and belligerent mechanisms.

"Test yer ability ter dodge?" invited a one-eyed android with a handful of sharp knives.

"Later on, Smiler." Piper led me through the crowd toward a booth in the far corner.

"Ah, how sad for you, Michel."

A guy had just come stumbling backwards through the smoky atmosphere to land smack in the middle of an intense Indian wrestling match. Michel's companions, after expressing regret, plucked him off the tabletop and uprighted him.

"Chungwa! Chungwa!" bellowed the robot gorilla who'd tossed him. "Test your masculinity, bwanas?"

"I'll best you, you shaggy *bête!* Hold my beret, François."

"Have a care, Fernand."

"Everyone," I observed, "seems concerned about proving his prowess."

"That's the sort of clientele P.J.'s bistro attracts."

A stunning yellow-haired girl materialized out of a circle of young men. "So much for Alexandre," she said in a husky voice. "Care to try your luck, Slim?" She was gazing through the murk right at me.

I squinted. "She's an andy too, isn't she?"

"Exactly." Piper hustled me along.

"The record so far," announced the beautiful blonde mechanism, "is three orgasms in fifteen minutes. You look as though you ought to be able to beat that, Slim."

"Three in fifteen minutes, that's impressive," I said. "Have you ever had a . . . um . . . relationship with a robot, Piper?"

"Never felt the need, my boy," he answered. "Oops, we'd best wait a moment." He halted, nodding at the booth we'd been aiming at.

"What's wrong?"

"We'll wait until he changes color."

There was a pudgy guy sitting alone in the shadowy booth, hunched over, one hand clutching a plyopouch of steam beer. His skin was a blazing crimson color. Face, hands, every bit of flesh showing was a gleaming red.

"What's ailing him?"

Piper said, "He's angry over something. It'll pass."

"How do you know he's angry?"

"There's a color code. Red is hopping mad, green is envious, yellow is annoyed, and so on," Piper explained. "His name is Moody."

"He's our contact?"

"That he is."

"How come he can change color?"

"Moody was born and bred near the Bayeux Energy Complex. A radiation leak from a small accident there in 2011 had an odd effect on his somatic pigmentation centers."

"Real handicap, telegraphing your moods like that."

"I oft suspect Moody can control it to some extent, making his knack useful in conning people. I've seen him feign everything from fright to satisfaction to cinch a deal."

"He's pink," I pointed out.

"We'll delay a few more seconds."

There was a sudden crash behind us. I spun in time to catch a glimpse of Fernand disentangling himself from the top tier of a pastry cart.

"Chungwa! Chungwa!" The triumphant robot gorilla beat on his hairy chest.

"You think," I asked Piper, "this is the best spot in Paris for a quiet chat?"

"While I can name five or six choicer locations, Moody favors P. J. Mechanix'."

"What does blue mean?"

"He's neutral," said Piper. "Come along. Ah, good evening, Moody."

"Far from it." He frowned up at us, turning briefly pink. "I suppose you've come barging in here with the idea of crowding into my private booth."

"Briefly, yes."

"Okay, just so you both plant your duffs on the other side," Moody instructed. "I don't like people too near me."

I murmured, "You picked the wrong place for isolation."

"What was that jibe, schmuck?" He flared red.

"I was mentioning as how—"

"Justin was lamenting the sad fact we're on such a tight schedule this trip," cut in Piper. "Otherwise he'd love to challenge the rowdiest robots in this joint. He's a very tough lad, I can vouch for that."

The red gave way to green and then a chill blue. "How do you plan to impose on my good nature this time, Piper?"

"I have to contact them," Piper said quietly.

Moody turned a deep purple. "They're all too damn busy for you. They've no time to do favors for outsiders."

"Moody, my lad, Piper never begs favors. I pay for them."

"How much?" His plump face was a gleaming green.

"The usual fee."

"Prices are going up, Piper. Cost of living's on the rise again, overhead grows."

"Where are they, Moody? I know they move around a lot, which is why they use you as an agent."

He went orange in the face. "Use me is right," he complained. "Simply because they don't think my gifts are as valuable as theirs. I'm treated like a sorry drudge, a poor relation who—"

"Their location."

Moody faded to a pale blue. "If I tell you, will you bap off and let me brood and suffer in peace?"

"A promise."

"They're temporarily holed up in a drafty old château in the Loire Valley," Moody told him. "The name of the pile is Château Restif."

"Farewell." Piper and I stood up. "We'll remember you in our prayers, Moody, my lad."

"Fat lot of good that'll do," he said, turning green.

CHAPTER 20

Piper noticed it first. "Wine bottle at eleven o'clock," he announced, nodding at the midday sky outside our skycar.

It was my turn at the controls, I'd been watching the forests and vineyards unrolling beneath us. Glancing in the direction indicated, I saw an enormous purple wine bottle, or rather a skyvan shaped like a wine bottle, flying in the same general direction we were. On its side throbbed, in electroglo letters, the words *Balbec Wineries! We Give You Extraordinary Vin Ordinaire!*

"Only a flying advertisement," I concluded.

"They've been traveling fast enough to overtake us." Rubbing at his moustache, Piper frowned. "Yet now they've slackened their speed, to keep close to us."

"Could be they want to give us a discount on a case of their wine."

"We'll shortly find out."

The cork end of the bottle popped open, it served as the lid of the control compartment. Two hefty guys in black one-piece fatiguesuits emerged, with an assortment of laserguns and blasters in their gloved fists and skybelts strapped to their broad backs.

"These fellows don't look like your typical wine merchants," I observed.

"Damn, I would rent an unarmed skycar. Figured this to be a pleasure jaunt." Snorting, he reached behind his seat into his duffel bag. "Even though I can't do much harm with a stungun, I'll give her a try." He spun it twice around his trigger finger.

The two men had flown clear of the flying wine bottle, were zooming straight at us.

"Something I'd like to try first," I said.

I hunched closer to the control panel, threw our skycar into manual, took over the flying entirely. We bucketed some, then straightened out.

Not for too long, since I began executing loops and banks all over the French afternoon.

In less than a minute I'd zigzagged us above the two attackers, who were making perplexed circles below.

"Excellent flying, my boy," said Piper. "My stomach will join me in praising you soon as it returns to my body."

I went diving right at one of the guys in black.

As it turned out, I concentrated too much on him.

His partner, and the first I was aware of it was when our ship started bleeping in alarm, was able to throw a laser shot or two right into the belly of the skycar.

The satisfaction I was feeling from scaring the one attacker into a series of lopsided somersaults faded when I realized we were well on our way to being disabled.

"Sounds as though they've sabotaged something fairly vital." Piper gazed down between his legs.

"Power source on these damn GMFords is under there. Stupid place to put it."

"Lads in the Detroit Redoubt probably weren't anticipating attacks by hostile wine bottles."

"Going to have to set down, Piper, otherwise we may smash up."

"Pick us a secluded spot where we can make a stand against these lads," he suggested. "If it's pleasant enough, we might possibly have a picnic afterwards."

The skycar was lurching, making odd whamming

sounds, losing altitude in shivery swoops. I fought with the controls, managed to guide it into a moderately smooth descent pattern.

The tops of the pine trees—I think they were pines—grew swiftly up to meet us. I skimmed along over the forest, then dropped the rattling skycar down into a small clearing.

Too small, it turned out. We went wooshing clean across it, slamming into a stand of sturdy old oaks with many impressive thumps and screeching rents.

"Out, quick!" Piper tossed me a spare stungun. "Get in among the trees."

"I've lost track of those bastards. Where are—"

The door on my side of the cabin suddenly melted right away. Framed in the heat haze left behind was a big guy in black, a lasergun in one hand and some kind of ugly blaster in the other.

"Which one of you mugs is Brinkman?" he inquired.

"Brinkman?" Piper gave him a perfect Boy-have-you-made-a-mistake #3. "My good man, I happen to be none other than Théophile Gautier, from the Ministry of Cheap Wine. The lad who so ably saved us from your rude attack is named Villiers de l'Isle—"

"Shut your blinkin' gob!" advised the second black-clad man. He'd just landed next to his comrade, his skybelt was still huffing. "'At young whelp's the one we wants, Alfie."

"Would that be a British accent I detect?" asked Piper, very slowly starting to raise the hand with the stungun in it. "What part of Merry Old England do you hail—"

"Me bloomin' orders don't call for punchin' your ticket, gov. Howsoever, I'll do it certain less you button your bloomin' bazoo. An' drop 'at stunner."

Piper lowered his gun hand. "I'd still like to mention what a lamentable mistake you lads are making. The

French Government, for which we both labor, will go hard on you. You've already violated several—"

"Might as well fry 'em both, Harchie."

"'Fraid so, Alfie."

Both of them raised their right hands, the hands with the blasters in them.

Then they both made queer popping sounds and ceased to be there. The air crackled and shimmered for several seconds around where they'd been standing.

"Hope those goops like Cincinnati."

Leaning against a nearby tree trunk, arms folded under her impressive breasts, was a tall blonde young woman. I suppose I shouldn't have been noticing how perky her nipples were a moment after I'd been saved from the jaws of death, except I was. She wore a pair of off-white slax, a pullover tunic with the word Gypsies emblazoned across it.

Piper allowed himself a small sigh. "Willow, my child, it's jolly running into you again." He backed out of our disabled skycar.

"Sorry I was so darn late," she apologized, smiling at him. "Sometimes these damn hunches don't come in quite as clear as I'd like."

"You sensed what was happening?"

"What was going to happen, sure," she replied. "Trouble is, took me almost ten minutes to get the damn location. Then I almost got lost flying here from the château."

Very carefully I let myself down on the sward. "Those guys," I said, "where are they?"

"In far-off Ohio, and probably feeling darn sorry for themselves about now. You ever been in Cincinnati?"

"Nope, never."

"I grew up there." She shrugged. "For a second there, before I teleported those goops, I was really tempted to send them right straight to my Aunt Sharon's parlor.

That'd fix 'em good. She'd make them throw away their guns, wipe their feet and help her rearrange the furniture."

"Justin, this fetching lass happens to be Willow Zainish." Piper put a fond hand on her bare tan shoulder. "One of the world's best precogs, and a highly efficient telek to boot."

"Wasn't much call for that sort of gift around Cincinnati." She, smiling, held out her hand to me. "I departed soon as I could, shortly after puberty hit me. Ended up with the Gypsies. Darn lucky for me."

"Could you," I asked while shaking her smooth warm hand, "get those fellows back here? I'm curious about who hired them."

"Heck, they're nothing but a couple thugs for hire," Willow told me. "Besides, I can tell you who paid them to try to kill you."

"Who was it?"

"Your family," she replied. "Yep, looks like the Kingsmills want you dead."

CHAPTER 21

There was a portly priest spread out on his back in the center of the vast Oriental carpet. The lightning that was crackling outside the thick stained-glass windows illuminated his plump face, turning it electric shades of blue, green, and red.

"Darn." Willow stopped with us at the doorway. "Never know if he's in one of his trances or tipsy."

Touching my arm with a wait-here gesture, the blonde hurried into the immense château library. Kneeling beside the sprawled priest, she sniffed at his lips.

She smiled and stood. "Not a whiff of booze," she announced, pleased. "Father Brown's only using his astral body to gather news and information." She beckoned us into the library.

The ceiling was high, sliced across with thick dark beams of real wood. Faded tapestries, celebrating battles won centuries before, hung down the stone walls between the high, crowded bookshelves.

"What denomination is he?" I asked, skirting Father Brown on my way to an ornate carved wood couch.

"He got himself defrocked years ago." Willow invited me with a plump at the cushion to sit closer to her. "Father Brown is what they used to call a whisky priest. Well, really he was a whisky priest, a gin priest, a wine priest and an anything else with a trace of booze in it priest."

"The good father's extrasensory gifts didn't much

impress the church fathers, either." Piper settled into an armchair.

"He tried to pass it off as a gift of god," said Willow. "They were more inclined to consider it demonic possession. Then when he went and installed the wetbar in his confessional, they lowered the boom. Tossed him clean out, excommunicated him, even canceled his hospitalization."

"Fortunately he wandered into the Gypsies," said Piper, "where his talents have been able to flourish."

"How many of you are there?" I asked the pretty Willow.

"Lots," she said. "We have affiliate Gypsies spotted all over the darn world. Here at the château we have just under a dozen. We'll likely be moving on soon, since there are a good many folks who don't take kindly to us."

"Speaking of rubbing people the wrong way," I said. "Why did you say it was my family, the Kingsmills, who are trying to kill me?"

"Didn't you get almost charbroiled by their minions?"

"How'd you link those guys up with the Kingsmills?"

"Father Brown did that," she said, pointing at him with a foot. "He found out during one of his trances last evening."

"But they didn't want to kill me before," I said. "How come now—"

"Seems like you've upset them. Chasing people to South America, generally making a fuss," she said. "The way I understand it, if you'd stayed planted in the Nabes they wouldn't have been concerned about bumping you off, Justin. Now they're afraid you're going to blab what you know."

"What the hell is it I'm supposed to know?"

She shook her head. "Father Brown had to bring his astral body on home before he found that out." Smiling, she delivered a friendly pat to my nearest knee. "Don't you worry, though, the Gypsies'll help you find out all you need to know."

"He may not be up to it."

A lean man came rolling into the room. He was about thirty-five or so, skin deeply tanned and hair a premature white. His wheelchair was hooked up to him in several places, with tiny tubes and wires reaching out of it and into his body. His two-piece neotweed worksuit had several small vents in it to allow for their passage.

Everything except his head was stiff and unmoving. His body never moved, you could hardly even detect his breathing. His gaunt, weathered head, though, turned from side to side, his eyes rarely rested.

Piper stood, waved him a greeting. "Oscar Shay, my boy, I appreciate your helping us out."

"We help anyone who can afford our fees." His silvery chair avoided the collapsed Father Brown as he wheeled closer to the couch I shared. "It will be very rough."

"What?"

"They did a lot of messing around with your mind," Shay told me. "I can probe, I can help you remember. The process is going to be very tough on you, very difficult to take. I'm frankly not sure you—"

"I need to find out more about who I am," I said. "I have to know why they did this to me. Doesn't matter how rough it gets."

Shay's left cheek hollowed, a faint smile touched his lips. "We'll start this evening then, after dinner."

Thunder rumbled outside, the wind brushed hard at the windows.

Father Brown came bobbing up to a sitting position. "My, my," he said, "you'll never guess where I've been."

CHAPTER 22

The room was high up in the château, its windows were narrow and leaded, the stone ceiling slanted sharply. Rain pounded against the windows' patchwork of colored glass, the wind whispered over the tile rooftops above us.

"I'm ready," I said.

Shay's chair brought him nearer the leather armchair I was, somewhat uneasily, sitting in. "Dr. Clarenson's a very thorough man," he began. "I've undone two of his other creations. The work was neither easy nor pleasant."

"So you implied before dinner." I shifted in my chair, found my backside was sticking to the real leather.

"Tonight I'll put you under," Shay said through barely moving lips. "We'll do some preliminary exploring. You'll start to remember a few things. Those true memories'll be the first hints of what's buried in your skull. The more I work with you, the more you're going to remember."

"Let's commence."

That faint, hollow smile of his appeared. "I'm not quite finished with my preamble, Justin," Shay said. "Clarenson and his stooges tried very hard to wipe out what you once were, but there's no foolproof way to do that permanently without resorting to drastic surgery. No work of that kind was done on you and, therefore, everything you were, all that you ever experienced, is still filed away in your brain. They tried to seal it up, put as many barriers as they could between your true past and you. When I start digging, at first anyway, you're going to be on their side. You—"

"Why would I—"

"Because they've planted all kinds of blocks, things to make you oppose anyone who attempts to unlock your past. They've programmed you so you'll feel good fighting me, bad about letting me in," Shay explained as he sat stiffly in his wheelchair. His eyes caught mine. "What you have to do is relax. Relax as much as you can, don't struggle against this. Don't fight at all . . ."

His eyes glowed in the dim room. The sound of the heavy night rain slowly faded.

"Relax . . . rest . . . trust me . . ."

Shay's voice turned into a faint buzzing. I seemed to be floating away from him, backing down an endless tunnel. His eyes . . .

Initially there was only blackness. That and pain, a gut-grabbing pain that scared the hell out of me. Somebody wanted to do something not at all good to me. I had to stop it, fight. The pain grew worse, worse, worse. There was nothing but pain. On and on. But then . . .

". . . parlor magic."

"And this?"

The empty glaz chair rose straight up from the office floor until it was dangling high above my Uncle Coulton's bald head. "There are a good many people in the world with telek powers, Kubert."

Bernie Kubert laughed through his thin nose. "Do they also have the ability to do this, Mr. Kingsmill?"

He cocked his right hand, pointed up at the chair.

The chair began to sputter and crackle. Bitter yellow smoke came puffing out of its joints. Then it blurred to dust. The shape of it held for a few seconds before drifting to the floor to form a glittering little mound of dust.

"Somewhat more impressive," admitted Uncle Coulton in that throaty voice of his, a voice that made you want to urge him to cough. "Hardly sufficient to—"

"We need you, need the Kingsmill organization." Kubert was acting a hell of a lot more aggressive than he'd even seemed on the newscasts. "Specifically we need the Grub operation. Therefore, we're prepared to treat you all very well."

"You really are goofy," my uncle told him.

I was not supposed to be hearing or seeing any of this. What nobody in the family was aware of was that I'd set up a small monitoring room for myself in one of the unused storerooms of the New England office and factory complex. Always pretty good with my hands and with things electronic, like my father I guess, I'd worked out a viewing setup which fed off the plant and office security surveillance system. Had to add a few minicams of my own, so I could keep tabs on Uncle Coulton and Uncle Lew. Lately, ever since my sixteenth birthday, I hadn't quite trusted them.

"I've saved the most convincing proof for last, Mr. Kingsmill," Kubert was saying up there on one of the small viewscreens I'd mounted on the brix wall. "I'll let you see me as I really am. That . . ."

". . . not going to do anything of the sort," my father said, angry.

Uncle Coulton ran a hand across his bare head, as though he still had hair to smooth down. "Do you realize the money and power this means for us?"

"We've sufficient money and power now, Coulton."

"Nothing like this, Dave."

Uncle Lew said, "It's so damn simple. We add this one,

absolutely undetectable, ingredient to Grub and gradually . . ."

Uncle Coulton was going to kill him.

He raised the blaster to fire.

I was in my storeroom, monitoring away. Sure, I'd rigged things so I could hear and see them. But there was no way I could communicate back.

Even so I yelled, "Look out, Dad! They're going to kill you!" as I went dashing out of there, along the endless corridors to where . . .

". . . cooperate, please?"

My head hurt, my stomach hurt. I was naked, crouched on the floor of a white room, shivering, unable to keep my teeth from clacking. Even though I was on the floor, I felt afraid I could fall still farther. Down and down. "Go to hell."

"If you cooperate," Beth promised, "I won't have to use this on you again, Justin."

"That's not my name. My name is . . . it's . . . Joshua . . . Yeah, I'm Joshua Kingsmill."

"I'm sorry." She came toward me with the shockstik.

"Not too bad."

For a moment I thought I had contracted some kind of pox. My arms were thick with goose bumps, my head was jiggling as though a chill had hold of me. Inside of me a lot of swirling and gurgling was going on.

"We'll try again tomorrow."

There was Oscar Shay, rigged in his chair, his eyes faded down to normal.

"I . . . I remembered some things."

"Yes, I know. You told me as you relived them," he

said. "We're only coming up with fragments so far, they're significant fragments, however."

"I saw them kill my father," I said. "I'm still not certain why they did it."

"We'll find out," Shay promised.

CHAPTER 23

As I crossed the broad sunlit terrace, Willow came running over to give me a warning.

"Justin," she said, catching hold of my sleeve, "I've just seen something else."

"Bad?"

Her pretty head bobbed up and down. "Woke myself up at the crack of day with a new darn vision," she said. "I saw that nasty uncle of yours . . . what's his name?"

"Coulton would be the nasty one. Lew's more in the jerk category. What'd you see?"

"He's very dissatisfied with the people he's hired to get rid of you so far," Willow said. "He's decided to hire the best, namely Vulko McNulty."

"Vulko McNulty, the highest-paid assassin in the world," I exclaimed. "But, sure, my uncles are involved in something vast. They can afford to go first cabin."

"I'm trying to tune in on McNulty himself. Thus far with not much luck. I'm really ticked off at myself," she said. "Soon as Father Brown gets back from his present projection, I'll put him to work on it too."

"Listen, Willow, I've seen this McNulty guy on television often enough," I said, attempting an unconcerned smile. "I'll be able to spot him before he gets near enough to—"

"That's just it, he never appears as himself on an actual job," she told me. "He's a master of disguise. I mean, darn, he could show up looking like a spitting image of me or Piper or even old doddering Father Brown."

"Wouldn't you sense something like that?"

"I might, except I'm not always one hundred percent accurate. More's the pity."

"I've got to meet Piper down in the gardens for a chat," I said. "I'll see what he thinks about this."

"I better tag along so—"

"This'll be a private conference."

She hesitated, biting at a thumb knuckle. "Okay, but be darn careful."

"I've been that for years now, Willow." Smiling, I continued on my way.

The formal gardens spread across more than three acres. There were flower beds, hedges, metal benches, enough marble statues to stock a small museum. The statues were of gods and goddesses, naked most of them but very sedate-looking nonetheless. Since the Gypsies didn't go in for gardening, there were as many weeds as flowers and the hedges had rippling uneven tops.

I found Piper slouched in a white metal chair, contemplating a slightly askew sundial. "O time too swift," he said, "O swiftness never ceasing."

"Feeling philosophical?"

"Reading the inscription on yonder time device, my boy."

I settled into a chair facing him across a patch of high grass. "These past four days have been damn interesting."

"So Oscar informs me."

"As of now, I've pretty much unlocked everything," I said. "Last night was exhilarating as hell. I got back my entire childhood. My mother, all the toys I had, the first girl I slept with. I lost my virtue at eleven."

"Congratulations."

I took in a deep breath, slowly let it out. "I know why

they dumped me. Why they tried to destroy my memories. What they're planning."

"I brought you here, Justin, to discover precisely this."

"You know part of it already," I said. "Still I'd like to go over the whole mess. Then we can figure out what steps come next."

"Proceed," he invited.

"I'm alive mostly because of Uncle Lew. Jerk that he is, he had qualms about killing me. Once I barged in on their killing of my father, and told them what I'd been finding out about their plans, they knew something had to be done," I began. "Uncle Coulton wanted to rig things so it'd look as though my father and I died in an accident at the same time. Lew argued him out of that. They let me live, but they called in Dr. Clarenson. He processed me. Then they gave out a fake story about my dying, had me dropped in the Chicago Nabes. Uncle Lew has some sentimental feelings about the family, plus which he was uneasy about the idea of murdering a teenager, a child almost. My father's death they covered up for weeks, making it look as though he died long after I supposedly had."

"What about the reason for all this duplicity? You've had only glimmers thus far."

I leaned forward, resting an elbow on my knee. "Listen, this is going to sound strange and probably incredible, Piper," I said. "Still, it's all absolutely true. This Bernie Kubert guy, who amuses people by claiming to be an alien from another planet. He really is."

Piper straightened up. "Eh?"

"Bernie Kubert is one of two hundred and ten aliens who teleported here from a distant planet named Esmeralda some nine years ago," I explained. "Actually, he's not humanoid at all. He's able to assume an acceptable shape in—"

"His shape isn't all that acceptable."

"Part of the act, so you'll figure he's nothing more than a simpleton who's harmless as hell," I said. I puckered my lips, wrinkled my nose. "To convince my uncles of what he really is, Kubert dropped his disguise for a moment. Uncle Coulton fainted. And there isn't a colder, more unreachable bastard in the world than him."

"What are our visitors really like?"

I said, "Kubert looks like something more suited for life deep underwater. Except his skin is crusty, spiky, sort of like coral in a way. His eyes, and he's got three of those, are . . . Well, let's simply say the Esmeraldans will take some getting used to."

"What's their real purpose for coming to Earth? It's bound to be more than the tourist impulse."

"They're the forerunners of an invasion force," I explained. "Kubert heads a group responsible for softening us up for the real invaders. To do that they need the Kingsmills. Specifically, they need Grub."

"That swill? What on earth for, my boy?"

"In order to repeat the method they've used successfully to conquer two other planets so far," I answered him. "They've developed a terrific new drug. Tasteless, colorless, odorless. This stuff works on the brain in a specific way. Softens you up, makes you feel kindly toward aliens, especially ones from Esmeralda who look like big walking chunks of dried-out undersea life."

Piper stood and locked his hands behind his back. "You're telling me, lad, they've been shooting this mind control drug into Grub."

"Yeah, which is why more and more folks of late have been saying nice things about alien invasions. Even Wildman Woolinsky is not against the notion."

"All because of Grub?"

"You find Grub in every damn civilized country on Earth. It's the best-selling synfood there is," I went on. "Our Kingsmill researchers long ago showed that in most developed countries over ninety-six percent of the population has tried Grub at least once. Seventy-five percent eat the stuff once a month or more. Put your mind control drug into Grub, you're going to reach one hell of a lot of people. And in the less rich nations, in Africa and India, our very own U. S. Government is sending in tons of Grub to feed the starving. Same thing, we know, is going on in South America. Kingsmill's also come up with a new Infant Grub for the less fortunate countries. Use it in place of formula. Okay then, over the past three years since my dad was murdered and I was erased, the Kingsmill clan and the aliens have made sure this mind control ingredient has been introduced into the systems of a goodly portion of the world's citizens, from old codgers to babes in arms."

"Praise the lord, I've always loathed Grub in any shape or form," said Piper. "But what of you, lad? You've been gulping down great quantities for years. Are you going to commence spouting off-planet ideologies or—"

"We Kingsmills are immune. Uncle Coulton saw to it we got a neutralizing shot, unbeknownst, before they started adding the control ingredient to the Grub supply."

"Then we won't be found licking the boots of our conquerors, you and I. Or do they have any feet to put boots on?"

"Nobody's going to conquer us," I said. "My father wouldn't go along with his brothers on this and they killed him. They thought I was out of the picture for good and all. I'm not, though, and I'm going to stop them."

"A shame you've been able to remember so much, lad," said Piper. "Otherwise they might have let you live."

There was a kilgun in his right hand. It was pointing at my chest.

"Hey! What the hell are you doing, Piper?"

"Oh, I'm not Piper," he said.

CHAPTER 24

A gun hummed.

"Shit," remarked Vulko McNulty. He stiffened, unable to pull the kilgun trigger.

His legs, first the left and then the right, went soft and jiggly. He genuflected on the white gravel of the path, toppled over, hit with a gritty thud.

"I'm a little late," apologized Beth.

She was, very slim and pretty, standing next to a marble Diana. Her stungun was dropping back into its holster.

"This part of your Federal Overseers job?" Squatting, I tugged at the Piper moustache McNulty was wearing. It came free.

"Piper's okay," Beth told my back. "I found him trussed up beneath the grape arbor yonder. Vulko used a stungun on him. We—"

"Why're you here?"

"To save your bacon, damn it."

I straightened, still not looking at her. "Thanks."

"He was hired to kill you," she said quietly. "I didn't want that to happen."

"Is that official FO policy?"

"Don't know. I've retired."

"You planning to go back to helping your dad prod his subjects with a shockstik?" I faced her.

"You remember now."

"Yeah, all of it, Beth," I said. "Everything your father

did to me to rub out my identity. Everything you did to help him."

"I'm sorry."

"Well, great. That'll give me back the three years you took out of my life, make up for what happened to me in the goddamn Nabes."

"What I was back then, I'm not now. Although you maybe don't believe that," she told me. "When FO got word what the Kingsmills had arranged with Vulko McNulty . . . well, I decided I had to stop that."

I watched her for a few silent seconds. "Christ, what a hopeless idiot I am. Looking at you again, Beth . . . Hell, I still love you."

"Same here."

"I don't even think I trust you."

"Suppose not."

Shaking my head, I walked close to her. "Do you know what they're up to, my uncles? What their real plans are?"

"No," Beth answered. "I'm fairly certain it's something nasty. Do you know now?"

"Yeah," I said. "It's something, if I can, I have to stop." That made me, unexpectedly, laugh. "Here I can't spot a disguised assassin, yet I'm talking about saving the whole damn world."

Very tentatively, she touched my chest with her fingertips. "I'd," Beth said, "like to stay with you."

"That's what you'll do then," I said. "Let's see about reviving Piper. After which I'll fill you both in on what I've been remembering."

"But first . . ." she said.

She pressed into me and I kissed her.

CHAPTER 25

Piper, the real Piper, wobbled. "I'm a trifle disappointed with my vaunted recuperative powers," he mentioned while en route to a big armchair in the château library. "Stunned early this morn, still jake-legged at sundown." He slumped into the chair.

Father Brown was squatting on the thick carpet in front of the deep stone fireplace. "Ought I to go now?"

"Wait for Oscar," advised Willow. She was alone on a tufted hassock in a dim corner of the room, not much looking in my direction.

I was sitting on the carved wood couch with Beth. "What did Vulko McNulty have to say?" I asked Willow.

"Nothing we didn't already know," she answered, very curtly I thought.

"Quite simply, your relatives want you dead." Oscar Shay's wheelchair carried him across the threshold to the center of the lofty library. "You're capable of tossing an enormous spanner into their whole scheme."

"We'll have to move soon." Willow folded her arms under her breasts. "Once they realize McNulty failed and we've got him, they'll make another try—a more ambitious one that could mean a whole darn lot of trouble for all of us."

I got to my feet. "No reason for you to put—"

"Be seated, my boy," advised Piper. "We've already agreed we're going to work on this matter as a team. After all, the future of civilization as we know it is at stake. I also think there's a chance to make a nice piece of change out of the situation eventually."

Shay, head twisting toward Father Brown, said, "Find out how long we have before the invaders intend to make their final move, reverend. We also need the control drug formula."

"My, I'll have a busy few minutes." Chortling, he arranged himself in a comfortable prone position in front of the fire. "I'll be back as soon as I can, my children."

The priest shut his eyes, folded his hands over his stomach. His feet jerked twice, then twice more. After which he was quiet and still, respiration running on low.

"Seems to me," I said, "the first thing to do is expose the damn Esmeraldans. I can do that through my media contacts, such as Twilight Ma—"

"You sure collect 'em, don't you?" said Willow.

"Less bickering." Shay's chair wheeled him over to me. "The aliens, with the help of your family, have been pumping the mind control formula into the world's population for nearly three years. Suppose the news media tells the world exactly what's been going on and what the plan is. Then minutes later Bernie Kubert appears on the screen, saying, 'Folks, ignore all that nasty talk. Listen to me, get set for a wonderful alien invasion you're really and truly going to love.' They may be far enough gone to heed his words."

"It's also a possibility lots of the media people, in light of their shabby eating habits, are chockful of the stuff as well," added Piper. "I note even our esteemed U. S. President, Mr. Wildman Woolinsky, was babbling kind words about Bernie and the invaders the other evening."

"I don't think they've got anyone completely under control yet," I said. "My notion is they have to feed the stuff into people for quite a spell of time. What I gathered when I used to eavesdrop around the family works backs that idea up. Twilight, for instance, doted on Grub and she sure wasn't under the—"

"You're not the greatest judge of womankind on the face of the planet," observed Willow.

"What I want to do," I continued, ignoring her, "is put together proof of what we know, then take it to Twilight Malone. She'll get it broadcast across the world. Her rating on the—"

"We can only do that after we do something to counteract the effects of the Esmeralda additive," Shay said.

Piper stroked at his moustache. "Can we counteract it, my boy?"

"I had Dr. Gottfredson teleported in," said Shay. "He arrived an hour ago."

"Gottfredson?" said Beth beside me. "Does he work for the Gypsies now?"

"For nearly a year," Willow said. "He's usually based in New Berlin."

Beth said, "We wondered what happened to him after he disappeared from the Alexandria Mind Control Center two years back."

Willow scowled across at her. "You better not have any notion about turning Doc Gottfredson over to those fascist buddies of yours, sis."

"I've quit the FO, lady. If you don't cease needling—"

"Lasses, the fate of the whole round world rests in our hands," pointed out Piper. "Let us not squabble on such a momentous occasion."

"Sorry," said Willow.

"Sorry," said Beth.

I said, "Once I'm inside the New England complex I can reactivate my spying system. They dismantled it after they caught on to what I was up to, but the skeleton's still likely to be there. I can tape some conferences between my crooked uncles and guys like Bernie Kubert. Footage that'll look terrific on a newscast."

"You can try that," said Shay, "after we do something about overcoming the effect of what they've been putting in Grub."

"Busting in there's too risky." Beth put her hand over mine. "They mean to have you dead. Step inside their territory and you're giving them a–"

"I'm an owner of the whole operation, remember?"

"Even so, they–"

"Don't fret so, sis," said Willow, recrossing her long legs. "With me to help him, Justin can pop right into that dump without anybody being the wiser. I'll make darn sure he makes it out again, too."

Beth shook her head. "It's too damn dangerous."

"Piece of paper. Piece of paper." Father Brown, eyes wide, was sitting up and patting at his clerical clothes.

Willow hurried over to give him a sheet of faxpaper and an electropen. "Get something good, rev?"

"We'll chat in a bit, my child." Biting at the tip of his tongue, Father Brown scribbled rapidly for a full five minutes. "There you are, Oscar, the formula for the mind control additive."

The chair brought Shay over to where he could read the sheet the elated priest was holding up. "Seems like a fairly simple formulation, except . . ."

"Except what?" inquired Piper.

"One of the ingredients is alien, some kind of mineral they apparently brought along from their home planet. Going to make our job tougher."

"But not impossible?" I said.

"No, we can do it. Simply going to mean more time and effort."

"They keep the formula locked within a very snug safe at the Mojave Desert facility." Father Brown rose, brushing at the knees of his rumpled black trousers. "Despite their villainy, Justin, your family runs a very neat and clean operation. Their Grub tubs are spotless, their soft drink vats spic and span. You wouldn't be afraid to eat their food, except for that poisonous additive."

"What about New England?" asked Shay. "Did your astral body pick up anything about a possible takeover date?"

Smiling, chortling, holding his hands to the fire, the portly priest said, "The good lord was truly with me this night, Oscar. I dropped in there at precisely the right time. None other than Bernie Kubert had stopped in to visit with Justin's two sinful uncles." He paused, rubbing his palms together. "The invaders believe, and a good deal of discreet field testing by the Kingsmill organization backs this up, that the people of our planet will be ready for takeover in approximately three months."

"Three months," said Shay. "Not a hell of a lot of time."

Willow said, "We can stop 'em with weeks to spare."

"Okay, first thing we do is break camp," Shay said. "We have to get out of the château."

I leaned closer to Beth. "Are you going to stay with us?"

"I'm going to stay with you," she answered.

CHAPTER 26

My techsuit was too tight under the arms. I was standing there on the night desert fussing with it.

"Gee, you sure got the fidgets," remarked Willow, who stood in the fuzzy shadow of a Joshua tree watching the distant cluster of huge domes which made up the main Grub processing plant.

"This costume doesn't fit quite right. I'm not jittery."

"It's the one your good friend Elizabeth sewed on," Willow said. "I whipped out mine, along with the perfect-fitting one Piper's clad in, in the time it took her to thread a–"

"Beth isn't a seamstress, so–"

"Dear cohorts," cut in Piper. "The midnight rec break, as specified in the last zealously contested contract twixt Kingsmill Industries and the Amalgamated Food & Beverage Technicians Guild, fast approaches. We must strike momentarily."

I fished out the rough floor plan I'd drawn from memory, unfolded the large sheet of faxpaper. "Okay, there's enough moonlight for one more quick look." I turned my finger into a pointer. "Willow, you set the trio of us down right here at the intersection of Corridor F and Corridor G. Can you hit that close to–"

"I can land you on a gnat's navel if I have to," she said with a sedate snort. "And I'm a darn good seamstress on top of that."

"The main syrup vats for SweetyPop are here in Wing

13, next to these secondary Grub processing rooms," I continued, tapping the sketch. "Piper, you and Willow slip into 13 at the agreed-on time and toss your anti-control gunk into Vats A1, A2 and B1."

"Understood, my boy." Piper smoothed his moustache with the hand that held the vial he'd brought from Europe.

Willow had a similar vial tucked between her breasts. "I still think you ought to come on into that darn syrup room with us, Justin."

"Nope, I've got to stand guard out in the corridor after I numb the security scanners for that area," I told her. "In case somebody comes along unexpectedly, I know enough about the Kingsmill operations to bluff them off."

"Attack time draws nigh," announced Piper. "By the way, my boy, why have you been feasting your eyes on me so intently since we teleported in from overseas?"

"Excuse it, Piper. Every once in a while I like to assure myself it's you and not a facsimile."

"There is one and only one authentic Piper. I am he," he said, grinning. "Indeed, I'm astonished you could have allowed that inept, and much thicker through the middle, McNulty to con you for even a—"

"Fellas, it's time, remember?" Willow took each of us by the arm. "Next stop, the intersection of F and G."

My techsuit got tighter, my vision blurred and faded out. My stomach whirled, my breath seemed to quit for a spell.

Then, seconds later, we were side by side in a long wall-lit corridor. Floors, walls, ceilings were tinted plaz, soft pale greens and blues. Mood music, gentle and soft, was oozing out of the hidden overhead speakers.

We had this patch of Corridor F to ourselves. "Go in and dump in exactly four minutes," I told them. "I'll meet you in front of Wing 13 in ten." I started away.

"That coat really looks awful from the back," Willow softly called after me.

The day before, at the defunct Riviera casino where the Gypsies had relocated, Oscar Shay and Dr. Gottfredson had perfected an additive that would wipe out, swiftly, the cumulative effect of the crap the Esmeraldans and my uncles had been feeding the world since I'd ceased to be Josh Kingsmill. It was a synthetic bacteria, capable of multiplying itself indefinitely. The thing is, it worked much more effectively when ingested in a liquid. Therefore, we had to introduce it into the SweetyPop syrup vats. Once in, it would keep on multiplying for weeks and weeks, assuring a constant and sufficient supply. I knew, as an heir to this whole setup, the vats weren't cleaned more than once every five or six months. Father Brown, or his astral body, had found out for us the next swabbing-out wasn't due for almost three months.

As you know, SweetyPop, which you can buy only at the Grub Huts, is the largest-selling soft drink there is. Besides which, this particular month Grub was giving a free glass to everyone who bought either a #2 Bucket of Grub or a Grubunny Sandwich. We'd calculated that, projecting from past sales figures, we'd be able to give just about everybody who needed one a dose of Dr. Gottfredson's wonder cure within the next two weeks.

All the SweetyPop used was made from syrup provided by the Mojave plant. The individual Huts added carbonated water.

My uncles, and to some extent my father, had always ignored me when I'd pointed out the security cameras in this plant weren't sufficient. Good thing they had ignored me.

Sneaking into an empty monitoring room, I was able to blank out the three cameras which were supposed to watch the syrup area. I accomplished that in under three and a half minutes. Meaning that when Piper and Willow entered Wing 13 nobody would see them. The cameras were blind; the six-man vat crew wouldn't be back from the level 3 rec area for another half hour.

I was feeling pleased and proud, even though my tunic was digging into my armpit, as I scooted back along the corridors toward Wing 13.

Then I walked around a bend and smack into my Uncle Lew.

CHAPTER 27

"How've you been?" my uncle asked me.

"Um . . . fine, just fine," I replied, stopping dead in my tracks. "All things considered."

"Glad to hear that." Uncle Lew had faded some since last we'd met. His hair was grayer, his skin pale and more wrinkled. He was by himself at the moment.

"Well . . ." I waited for him to yell for security people.

"You weren't here during my last visit, I don't believe." He was squinting into my face, thoughtful. "Although you do look vaguely familiar."

"I only recently arrived here, sir."

I'd forgotten something. Even though I was again Josh Kingsmill inside, my outside was the one that'd been stuck on me by Dr. Clarenson and his surgical aides. The reworking of my face and the three years of growing since had made me unrecognizable to Uncle Lew. Quite obviously Uncle Coulton would've recognized me, since he'd been able to tell Vulko McNulty, the famous assassin, what I was looking like at present and where I might be found. Uncle Lew, though, was the squeamish one and he wouldn't have wanted to know anything about what I was like now.

"Very nice talking to you, sir," I said. "I'd best be hurrying back to my post."

My uncle chuckled. "I'm very glad to find at least one of my employees who doesn't steal the full recreation period from me," he said approvingly. "What's your name, son?"

"Stonebridge, sir. Oliver Stonebridge."

"Well, Oliver, I'll see what we can do for you."

"Thanks a lot, sir." I gave him an obsequious salute, hurried off.

"Need more young fellows like that," I heard my uncle mutter as he continued on in the opposite direction.

"What're you doing in this area, mister?"

I was only a few yards from the pale peach portals of Wing 13. My inquisitor was a large guy in the black and silver uniform of a Kingsmill Security Cop. "Oh, did Mr. Kingsmill neglect to inform you?" I put an Innocent As A Babe #2 on my face.

He didn't lower the stunrod he'd raised on noticing me. "No," he said.

"I'm supposed to get him smear samples from the syrup vats."

"Why?"

I shrugged, gave him a very convincing, so I felt, I Only Work Here grin. "He only told me what he wanted done, not the reason." I eyed the wall clock. Piper and Willow ought to be stepping out of that door yonder in approximately ten seconds.

"You got a written order to that effect?" He eased closer, until the tip of the stunner was less than a foot from my chest.

"Gee, no," I admitted. "I ran into Mr. Kingsmill back in Corridor D just now and—"

"How about your Employee ID Packet?"

I laughed disarmingly, though it failed to disarm him. "I guess I had to have one to get through the gates tonight." I made no move to produce identification. We'd faked uniforms, but skipped ID papers.

"Let's see 'em, mister. And move slow."

"Mother always tucks the packet into my breast pocket while she's kissing me goodbye on our doorstep." I patted myself in various likely and unlikely places. "Then I take the packet out, show it to the guard 'bots at the gate. Gosh, where did I put the darn old thing thereafter?"

"You got yourself all of a half minute to recollect." The stunrod was shortening the distance between us.

"Oh, sure, I remember now."

The sec cop went pop. The air rushed in to fill the spot where he and the stunrod had been.

Out of Wing 13 came a grinning Willow. "Hope he likes Cincinnati."

"You really ought to stop sending everybody there," I told her. "You're going to clutter the—"

"Don't I get so much as a thankful hug and kiss for ridding you of him?"

"Well, sure, but—"

"No time for clinches." Piper had followed her into our corridor. "We must flit."

"Everything go okay?" I asked him.

"It went in usual Piper fashion," he said. "Perfectly."

CHAPTER 28

"We didn't need her along, I still say," said Willow.

"Hush," I advised.

The three of us, Willow, Beth, and me, were in one of the see-through corridors of the New England Kingsmill complex.

It was almost spring, the trees on our private acres were on the verge of budding. And crowded between all that awakening foliage were people, hundreds of them, all angry and shouting. Lots of them brandished signs scrawled over with belligerent expressions such as *Alien Lovers!* and *Kubert, Get Lost* and *No Aliens For Us!*

Let me pause a moment to explain about the why of those demonstrators. We'd dumped Dr. Gottfredson's new bacteria into the SweetyPop syrup supply three weeks earlier. By now the augmented soft drink had been guzzled in large quantities throughout the entire world. Somehow, and the doctor charged this was due to something Oscar Shay had contributed, the anticontrol ingredient was having an unexpectedly violent effect. People didn't simply become less favorably inclined toward an alien invasion, they grew extremely nasty about the whole idea.

Bernie Kubert's purloined letter approach, of hiding the fact he was an alien by claiming to be one, wasn't working well any longer. He was heckled and attacked everywhere he went. Citizens suspected of pro-alien feelings were frequently punched in the nose. Down in the

Mississippi Enclave a man suspected of being an alien had been tarred and feathered before being run out of town. Well, since they didn't have access to tar or feathers, they actually dipped the guy in corn syrup and rolled him in frosted cornflakes. The intent was the same.

Knowing Kubert was a frequent visitor to the Kingsmill complex and that Uncle Coulton had been making some very positive speeches about the benefits of alien visitations, a good many of the most aggressive newly created alien haters had broken through the sec system to surround the New England facility, waving their signs and shouting their displeasure.

"Doc Gottfredson overdid it," remarked Beth while we moved along the afternoon corridor toward the storeroom I wanted.

This was my second recent visit. Willow and I had popped in three nights earlier, long after midnight when there was only a small and drowsy security staff in the place. I'd succeeded, on that prior visit, in reestablishing my monitoring setup. I had a full dozen view screens working, with a vidtape box standing by.

We'd been alerted, thanks to Father Brown's astral person, that Bernie Kubert was due to visit my Uncle Coulton here this very afternoon. All I had to do was tape the conversation and I knew I'd have some nifty footage to pass on to Twilight Malone. I'd already been in touch with her, though that annoyed both Willow and Beth. I'd hinted at what I'd be able to provide and Twilight was anxiously standing by. I'd also urged her to drink plenty of SweetyPop while she waited.

I opened the door and went into the storeroom. Beth and Willow came after. There were my twelve screens, each showing a picture of some part of the complex and the grounds outside.

There, too, was Uncle Coulton.

Sitting on an empty Grub packing case, legs crossed, left foot slowly swinging from side to side. A stungun in the lap of his two-piece buff bizsuit.

"You aren't that much different, Josh," he said.

"Uncle Lew didn't tumble when I met him a few weeks back."

"Lew has a brain the size of a cockroach's left nut," my bald uncle said, smiling at the two girls.

"You knew I was coming," I said.

"Our security here is better than it was in your day," he said. "I knew about your last visit shortly after you made it. With the help of one of my newer and brighter computers, I calculated when you'd drop in again. Been waiting."

"You might as well forget about harming him, Mr. Kingsmill," Beth told him. "All you have to do is look at some of those screens up there to see your plans are kaflooey. People are turning against you all over the world."

"The Esmeraldans aren't going to make it," added Willow.

"Kubert and I have devised a new and much stronger additive." He picked up the gun. "Once that gets into the Grub and has a chance to—"

"We know too much about you, Uncle Coulton," I said. "See, I've gotten my memory back. I remember what you did to me . . . and to my father."

I must have taken a step toward him, because the gun swung up. "None of that matters," he said in his rumbling voice.

"Are you figuring to try to kill me right here in—"

"No, I'm going to leave that to Kubert," my uncle informed me. "He'll be here quite soon. He has some wonderfully efficient ways of dealing with difficult nephews.

He's also splendid with young ladies who should have minded their own business."

Beth all at once laughed. "Bernie Kubert isn't going to do anything much for you, Mr. Kingsmill." She inclined her head toward one of the view screens up on the wall.

I glanced at it in time to see Kubert turn to his true shape. That didn't help him, because when upwards of three hundred angry people jump you, it doesn't matter how gifted you are at killing. They'd attacked his skycar when it set down on the landing area, overwhelmed him and his guards.

Uncle Coulton couldn't resist taking a look at what we all were gazing at.

The instant he turned his head, I jumped. I got in a terrific sock to his jaw, then two punches deep in his midsection.

He gurgled, doubled, and then fell off his packing case. As he slipped by I kicked the gun from his grasp.

He slammed into the plaz flooring, sprawled into unconsciousness.

It was a very satisfying moment for me.

The sun is shining where I am now.

This is an island. I'd just as well not mention the exact location. Somewhere in the middle of the Atlantic, where the smattering of Portuguese I picked up in Ereguay is useful. From the terrace of the villa I'm renting I can see a rocky hillside, speckled with some almost tropical foliage, and then the ocean stretching away forever.

Been here since I left New England, devoting a good deal of my time to jotting down my memoirs.

I wanted to get this all down before it began to fade away from me. Up until a few months ago, I was going around with the wrong past. I want to savor the one I really own.

L28

I'm alone here. By choice. Wanted to write and think for a spell.

I came out at this end more optimistic than I went in. While I've been here the world, aided by the Gypsies, has pretty nearly eliminated the alien threat. I don't think the Esmeraldans will try to reestablish a base here. They prefer pushover planets.

As of today I still haven't quite been taken back into the bosom of the Kingsmill clan. Even though Uncle Coulton fled and is believed to be hiding out in one of the Alaskan Colonies, there are considerable cousins to contend with.

Piper is handling the negotiations with the family, helped out by three of the best shyster lawyers known to man. He's thus far managed to get me a sort of pension. More than enough to live on.

I don't intend to stay on this island much longer. I've done most of my thinking and remembering.

Next I want to get in touch with Beth.

Sure, I liked Twilight and I'm fond of Willow. But Beth . . . well, she's the only Beth there is.

Some of what happened between us wasn't that splendid. Still I lost her once and I don't want that to happen anymore.

When I finish this account, I'll head for where she is.

Listen, I'm fairly sure she and I can work out a pretty good life together.

More on that later.